Kings, Queens, Castles, and Crusades

Life in the Middle Ages

by Zelma Kallay

Good Apple

DEDICATED WITH ALL MY LOVE AND APPRECIATION

TO MY FAMILY AND ALL OF MY FRIENDS WHO HAVE GIVEN ME THE STRENGTH,

KNOWLEDGE, AND INSPIRATION TO WRITE THIS BOOK.

FOR WITHOUT THEM, NONE OF THIS WOULD BE POSSIBLE. THANKS AGAIN, MOM!

Editors: Suzanne Moyers
                    Susan Eddy

Designer: Michele Episcopo

Illustration: Doris Simone

Cover Illustration: Rosanne Guararra
                    Jennifer Hewitson

Good Apple
A Division of Frank Schaffer Publications, Inc.
23740 Hawthorne Boulevard
Torrance, CA 90505-5927

ISBN: 1-56417-666-5

2 3 4 5 6 7 8 9   03 02 01 00 99 98

Contents

Children everywhere are fascinated by knights, ladies-in-waiting, and castle technology. And, why not? After all, the history of the Middle Ages encompasses all the elements of great drama: political intrigue, pageantry, and romance.

This book is built around the minibiographies of medieval celebrities like Eleanor of Aquitaine and the poet Geoffrey Chaucer. Each biography is followed by several subchapters detailing relevant aspects of medieval life.

At the end of each chapter are reproducibles that invite students to explore everything from gargoyles to medieval herbs to fashions of the times. Children can calculate the provisions needed for a medieval feast, use homemade ink to illuminate letters as monks once did, and set up a merchant's stall. They can perform a play based on a Chaucer tale and learn about Muslim inventions brought back to Europe by zealous crusaders.

At the end of each chapter is a special project that explains, for instance, how to make candles or medieval musical instruments. Most of these projects require materials found in your kitchen or junk drawer.

At the end of the book, you'll find an answer key for many of the reproducibles, as well as a resource list of children's books, software, and games to enrich your medieval unit.

THE MIDDLE AGES INTRODUCTION

THE MIDDLE AGES
An Overview

The Middle Ages is the period of history between about A.D. 500 and 1500. The word *medieval*, which comes from the Latin *medium aevum*, or "middle era," is used to describe the Middle Ages.

The Middle Ages began after the fall of the Roman Empire. Between A.D. 400 and 800, a period often referred to as the Dark Ages, disorder reigned. Barbarian tribes from Germanic territories invaded. Communications and legal systems deteriorated. Nonetheless, this period was not entirely without promise. Cities such as Constantinople thrived as centers of commerce, culture, and political strength.

Around 800, King Charlemagne helped reunite Europe; building great libraries and schools of learning and encouraging the spread of Christianity. Organized religion helped establish law and order. After Charlemagne, King Otto of Germany helped staunch the invasions of northern aggressors. His dominion became known as the Holy Roman Empire because he was supported by the pope, in Italy.

For hundreds of years, various parts of Europe remained the target of outside invaders. During the Dark Ages these included the Magyars, from central Europe, and Saxons, Goths, and Franks, from northern and central Europe. Many invaders were defeated; others became assimilated into European society. Gradually, as a more systematic form of government evolved, England, France, and Germany became distinct countries. Even after medieval society became more organized, though, Viking war parties from Scandinavia wreaked havoc in Europe until late in the eleventh century.

After 1000, Europe became more stable. Trade brought new wealth to a greater number of people. Towns and cities flourished. The Catholic Church became one of the most powerful institutions in the world. It sponsored schools of learning and certain forms of artistic expression. But natural disasters, like famine and the dreaded black plague, as well as corruption in the Church and among feudal lords, led to discontent and change. Eventually, new ideas and scientific discoveries paved the way for the Renaissance.

William the Conqueror

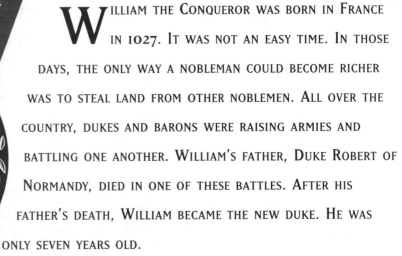

William the Conqueror was born in France in 1027. It was not an easy time. In those days, the only way a nobleman could become richer was to steal land from other noblemen. All over the country, dukes and barons were raising armies and battling one another. William's father, Duke Robert of Normandy, died in one of these battles. After his father's death, William became the new duke. He was only seven years old.

A King in Training

As he grew up, William studied very hard and practiced his battle skills with other boys. He also learned how to make armor, plow the fields, and take care of animals. All of these things helped him become an excellent fighter and leader. But being a king in training was also dangerous. Noblemen who wanted more land often tried to kidnap and even kill young dukes and princes. Some of William's own friends and relatives wanted to take his lands from him. Duke William once had to be hidden from would-be kidnappers in a pig sty on a neighbor's farm.

Still, William survived his childhood. By the time he was 24 years old, he had become the greatest lord in France. But William was not satisfied with his riches or his accomplishments. He wanted to rule England as well.

Making a Marriage

William's mother arranged for him to marry Matilda of Flanders, the daughter of the wealthy Count Baldwin of Flanders. Matilda was a highborn woman related to a famous English king named Alfred the Great. William understood that getting married to a woman with royal connections and money could help his career. The wedding was held in 1053.

One day, William discovered that his cousin King Edward of England was dying. Edward, who had no children, had once promised that William could become king after Edward died.

William rushed to England to remind Edward of this promise. Edward remembered and agreed that William should become king.

But many people did not want a French king to rule over England. After King Edward died, his advisers told everyone that Harold of Wessex had been picked as the king's successor.

THE BATTLE OF HASTINGS

Back in Normandy, William was furious. He decided that he would fight Harold to become the English king. On October 14, 1066, William invaded Hastings, England, with a huge army, including 300 young boys.

King Harold's army was not very strong. Many of his soldiers were fighting Viking invaders in another part of the country. And William was an intelligent warrior. He watched the English soldiers very carefully as they fought. William noticed that when one part of his army became weak, the enemy soldiers would swarm in to finish them off. This gave William and his remaining troops the opportunity to sneak up behind the other army and ambush.

WILLIAM THE ConQUEROR

Again and again, William and his soldiers pretended to retreat. Again and again, another group of French soldiers would surprise the English from behind.

After nine long hours of battle, William had won. All that could be seen on the blood-soaked hill where the battle had taken place was a lone apple tree and the bodies of many brave soldiers. Duke William marched on to London, the capital of England. He was crowned King of England on Christmas Day, 1066, and became known as William the Conqueror.

WILLIAM THE KING

During his reign, William ordered all the landowners in England to fortify, or protect, their lands from invaders by building big stone castles. He also promised the English people that he would not change their basic laws and customs. He made a few new laws that helped control the powerful feudal lords who were always fighting over their lands. This brought new peace to the kingdom. The English eventually thought of William as an excellent king.

Name _____

If You Were King William

Use some of the vocabulary at the bottom of this page to answer these questions.

1. You have just discovered that your father has died and you are to become the new duke. What is your first thought on hearing this news?

    _____

    _____

2. How would you feel if you discovered that your best friend was planning to fight against you for some of your lands?

    _____

    _____

3. How would you feel about having to marry someone that your parents picked out for you?

    _____

    _____

4. How would you describe the Battle of Hastings in a letter to your queen?

    _____

    _____

5. What is the first thing you would do or say to show the English people that, even though you were French, you would be a good king?

    _____

    _____

Vocabulary

battle	parcel	successor	highborn	tactics
reign	military	hostile	feudal	knight
loyalty	proclaimed	heir	armor	conqueror

THE FEUDAL SYSTEM

During his reign as King of England, William the Conqueror strengthened a system of government known as feudalism. This system helped keep order and peace during a difficult time in history.

BEFORE FEUDALISM

Before the feudal system most people in Europe lived under Roman law. The Romans were originally from Italy, but they conquered many lands outside their homeland. Roman government was not perfect, but it worked for many people over a long period of time. The Romans built roads and bridges all through Europe, started libraries, and created courts to settle arguments. Under Roman law some people even had the right to vote for their leaders.

But after hundreds of years, the Roman government became too spread out and complicated. On top of that, barbarians from other lands began to invade Roman territories. Many Roman governors and senators fled to Italy, leaving everyone else to take care of themselves.

Suddenly, important landowners found themselves fighting to keep their lands. They needed to find soldiers who could protect them. These soldiers eventually were called knights. In return for their loyalty, the king was expected to pay his knights a fee. The word *fee* comes from the Latin word for "payment," *feudum*. In England and France the word for "fee" was *fief* (feef).

Fiefs, Lords, and Barons

When feudalism first began, a knight's fief might be an award of armor, weapons, clothing, horses, or food. Later the fief became a parcel of land that the knight could live on as long as he continued to fight for his king.

A kingdom might be split up into about 50 fiefs. A knight had power over everyone who lived on his land. He could sell or trade the things the peasants grew on his land. This "chief knight" was later called a lord. The richest lords were called barons.

Sometimes a baron's land was too large to manage, so he would divide it into smaller sections on which other knights could live and farm. These knights would then swear an oath of loyalty to the lord who gave them the land. The knights living under the lord were later called dukes, earls, or counts, depending on how much land they owned. Other people who lived on the knight's land included bailifs, villeins and, at the bottom of the heap, serfs.

The Lowest of the Low

To understand the way medieval society worked, let's start with serfs, who were at the bottom of the feudal social pyramid.

Serfs were like slaves, toiling away for the lord, duke, or count. They worked from dawn to dusk, and received no money for their work. Serfs were not allowed to leave the lord's land. They could only become free by escaping capture for one year and a day. Serfs did receive food, clothing, and a small hut for themselves and their families. They also were promised protection during wars and invasions.

Slightly above the serfs in power were the villeins, free men who controlled very small plots of land. They could sell the things they grew, but could not sell the land itself. Villeins had to make payments to their lords in crops, animals, and anything else they produced.

Commoners were slightly better off than the villeins. This group included merchants who ran businesses in the community and servants who worked in the local castle or manor. The merchants worked near the castle or in the town and paid rent and taxes to the king. Castle servants did chores such as cleaning, cooking, making repairs, and other tasks. They were paid for their work in money, food, and clothing.

Servants to a Lord

A bailiff worked directly for the lord, collecting rent, taxes, and fines, and finding people to serve on juries. A bailiff could also serve as a judge for the commoners. On just about the same level as a bailiff was the viscount, an assistant to a count or countess. He managed all the people on the fief, their jobs, and the many problems that the counts and countesses did not have time for.

The counts answered to the dukes and the dukes answered to the barons. All the people "above" the merchants (not including Church officials) were called nobility.

Name _____

The Feudal Pyramid

Kings in feudal Europe had the most power, even though there were very few of them. Serfs had the least amount of power, even though they made up the largest portion of the population.

Directions

Cut apart these puzzle pieces and put them together to make a pyramid. What does this picture tell you about life for most people during this time?

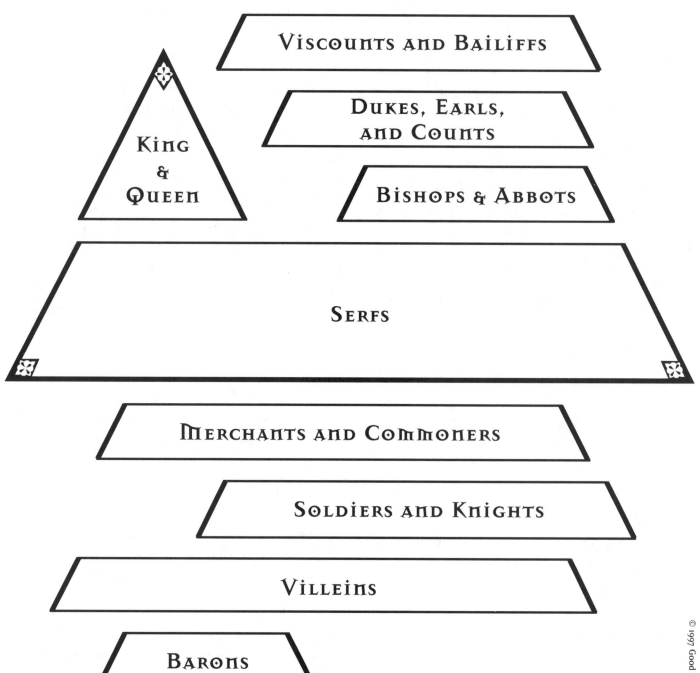

Name _____

WHO GETS WHAT: DIVIDING A FIEFDOM

DIRECTIONS

Each of the knights below have been awarded a portion of this imaginary land because they fought for their king. Use the map grid to show each knight's fief.

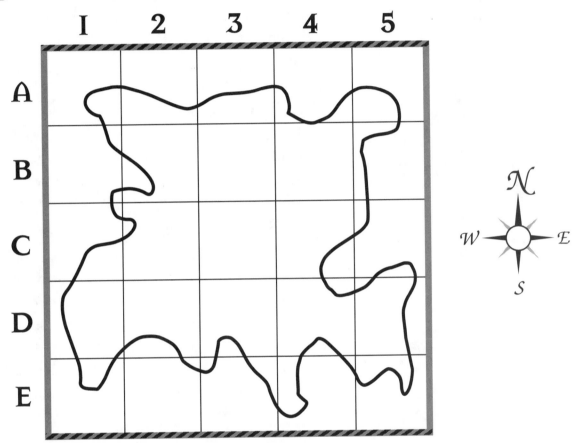

The Red Knight's fief spans from A1 to A3 in the north and from B1 to B3 in the south. Color his land RED.

The Blue Knight's fief spans from A4 and A5 in the north to C4 and C5 in the south. Color his land BLUE.

The Green Knight's fief spans from C1 to C3 in the north and from D1 to D5 in the south. Color his land GREEN.

The Orange Knight's fief includes the contiguous portions of E3 and E4. Color his land ORANGE.

Who got the biggest fief? _____

What might have been the reason that this knight got the most land?

_____

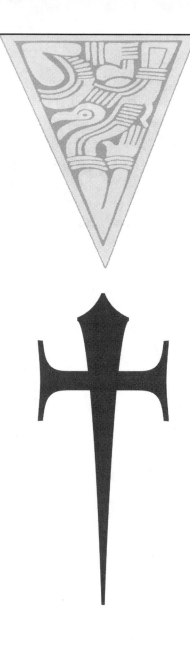

To Be a Knight

When he was a boy, William the Conqueror trained to be a knight. This gave him experience in fighting and leadership. Although all sons of noblemen could train to become knights, most would later serve a king or a lord—few *became* a king or a lord.

A Page's Life

Starting at about the age of seven, a noble boy could become a page to one of his father's knights. Pages were expected to study hard and learn manners, or etiquette, as well as how to care for a knight's armor and weapons.

To learn etiquette, a page spent a part of each day with the women of the castle. Noblewomen and queens taught pages how to play musical instruments, sing, and recite poetry. They also learned how to serve food to people who sat at the high table, usually the royal family. Because silverware hadn't been invented yet, pages brought bowls of water that diners could use to wash their fingers between courses.

Pages also spent time with monks, who taught them reading (and sometimes writing), arithmetic, geometry, and strategy games.

But the person the page spent most of his time with was his knight's squire. The squire taught the page to shoot a bow and arrow, train falcons, fight with a sword, and ride a horse. The squire also taught the page to joust, a medieval way of doing battle. To practice jousting, the page would learn to ride a horse while aiming a lance at a special target called a quintain. A quintain was a T-shaped pole stuck into the ground. If the page missed the target, it would quickly swivel all the way around, hitting him on the back of his head and knocking him off his horse.

The page was also a squire's servant. The page had to lay out the squire's clothes, heat and carry water for the squire's bath, help him get dressed, and wait on him during a feast. The page also polished the squire's armor.

A Page Becomes a Squire

At the age of 14, the page became a squire to one knight. This knight taught the squire how to make and fix weapons and armor. The knight also taught the squire complicated fighting techniques. During jousts and tournaments, squires assisted knights with their horses, spurs, and weapons. Eventually a knight took his best squires into battle with him.

At the age of 21, the squire was usually ready to be knighted. The evening before his knighthood ceremony, the squire would bathe and dress in a white gown. Then he would go to the church and pray. In the afternoon the squire dressed in a full suit of armor. Finally the squire's knight would give him his own special sword. Now the squire was ready to be dubbed a knight.

Getting Dubbed

During the dubbing ceremony a nobleman or priest would strike the squire on the shoulder with the flat side of a sword. Then the squire would swear to be brave, honest, humble, and courteous (especially to women) as well as helpful and generous to the poor and weak.

It was usually at this time that a new knight would be asked to swear fealty to one special person, such as a king, queen, or duke, as well as to his country. Swearing fealty meant promising to fight in battles or wars whenever asked or paying money to help support a nobleman.

Finally the new knight received a special pair of spurs, which might be fastened to his boots by his page or wife.

Fox and Geese: A Strategy Game✦

Cut out this game board and read the directions below to play a game that helped squires practice military skills.

To Prepare

- Make 13 markers of one size, color, and shape. These are the Geese.

- Make 1 marker of another size, color, and shape. This is the Fox.

- Place the Geese together on one side of the board.

- Place the Fox in the center of the board, facing the Geese.

To Play

- Fox goes first.

- Fox can move one space at a time in any direction along a line. Fox can jump over one Goose in any direction. He can make many jumps in a row. When Fox jumps over a Goose, he also captures it.

- Geese can only move one space at a time, along any line, in any direction. Geese cannot jump any pieces.

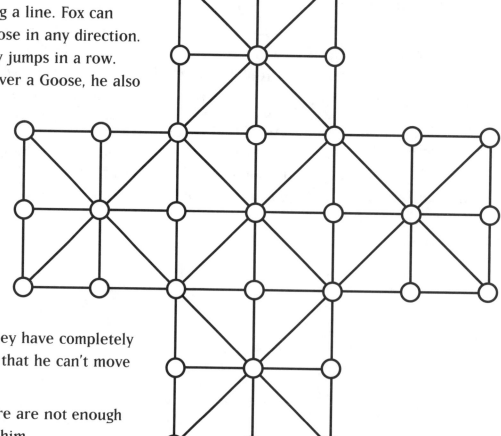

To Win

- Geese win when they have completely surrounded Fox so that he can't move or jump.

- Fox wins when there are not enough Geese to surround him.

✦ NOTE TO TEACHER: Enlarge the game board for easier play.

Name _____

Blazon Your Coat of Arms! ✦

During battle, knights wore visors that hid their faces. The design, or coat of arms, on a knight's shield helped others identify him. It included many symbols related to the knight's life and adventures.

Directions

Blazon, or add symbols to, the shield below by following the labels.

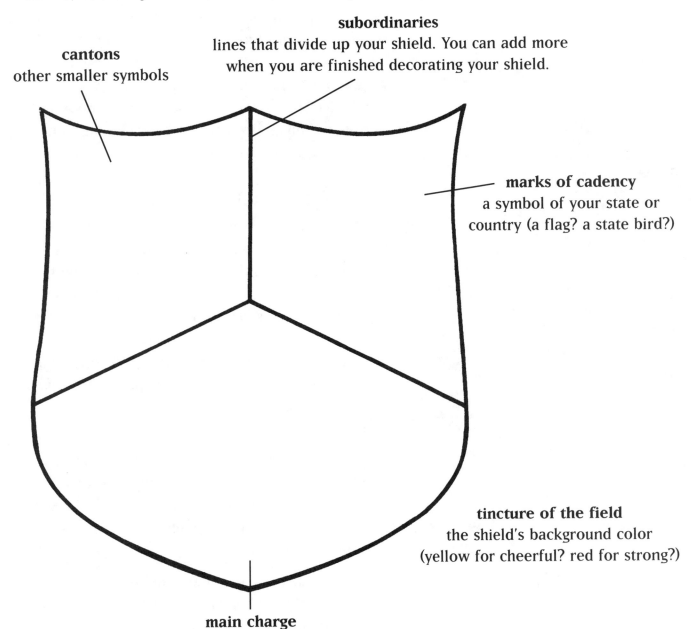

subordinaries
lines that divide up your shield. You can add more when you are finished decorating your shield.

cantons
other smaller symbols

marks of cadency
a symbol of your state or country (a flag? a state bird?)

tincture of the field
the shield's background color (yellow for cheerful? red for strong?)

main charge
a symbol representing something important about your life (a picture of your home? your best friend? a favorite book?)

✦ Note to teacher: Enlarge the shield to allow for more intricate designs.

THE
CASTLE OF A KING

One of the first things that William the Conqueror did when he became King of England was order all the noblemen to fortify, or strengthen, their castles. Up until then most kings and queens lived in wooden castles. The problem was that these castles were too easy to burn down. An invader would simply light his arrow and send it flying into a wall or tower. William decreed, or ordered, that all new castles be built with stone.

NEW CASTLE TECHNOLOGY

As stone castles were built, other new things were added. Gatehouses were built between the lists, or outer grounds, and the moats that surrounded the castle. Now guards could sound the alarm if they spotted enemies nearby. Gatehouses were protected by a special door called a portcullis, which was made of heavy wood or iron and could be locked with huge metal bars. Because the portcullis was heavy, a smaller door alongside it was used for everyday activities.

Within the gatehouse entry were arrow loops, small holes in the walls for shooting arrows at the enemy. In the ceiling were "murder holes" through which boiling water or oil could be dropped onto enemy soldiers.

Wooden palisades, or outer walls, were replaced with stone walls called curtains. Each of these walls was about 300 feet long, 35 feet tall, and 12 feet thick. Along the wall's edges were lower walls called parapets. Inside the parapets were more murder holes. There were also guard towers along each wall.

A Look Inside

Just inside the castle walls was the bailey, where stables, servants' quarters, and shops were usually located. Here there might also be a fishpond that provided fish to eat, a place for children to play and swim, and water for putting out fires. There were also gardens, kitchen sheds, and huge stone ovens in this area.

Some stone castles had inner courtyards or inner baileys. The most important building of the inner bailey was the keep. The basement of the keep was used for storing food and important papers. Next to the basement was the donjon (dungeon), where prisoners of war were kept.

On the main floor of the keep was the great hall, a huge room used as a gathering place for the noble family and its guests. Here the king and queen heard news about their kingdom, gave banquets, and were entertained by minstrels, bards, and jugglers. The main floor usually housed a chapel and servants' rooms.

On the top floor of the keep was the royal chamber. This is where the king and queen, as well as children, servants, and dogs, would sleep or relax.

Capturing a Castle

These stone castles were a big improvement over wooden ones, but they weren't perfect. Stones hold moisture, so castles were often musty and cold. Because there were few windows, castle rooms were dark. Yet it was almost impossible for enemy soldiers to get into a well-fortified castle. Instead, armies would lay seige to the castle, camping outside the walls for weeks or even months. During a seige, supplies could not reach the people inside. Over time the people might begin to starve. Usually the enemy gave up or the people inside surrendered before that happened.

WHERE IN THE CASTLE ARE YOU?

DIRECTIONS

Read the quotes at the bottom of this page. Write a number next to the quote to show where in the castle each person is located. Circle the name of the person who might be speaking.

A) I check out every person entering or leaving the castle. We don't want any spies getting in to poison the king!

Location: _____

Speaker: chief porter   queen   squire

B) This is where I have my shop. I shoe horses, make spurs, and fit bridles.

Location: _____

Speaker: wheelwright   guard   blacksmith

C) I spend a lot of time serving my knight here during a tournament. I help him put on his spurs and I water his horse.

Location: _____

Speaker: page   guard   squire

D) During battle I position myself here. I can shoot my arrows outside, but the enemy can't shoot in.

Location: _____

Speaker: chatelaine   steward   soldier

E) As the castle's chatelaine, I spend time here directing my ladies-in-waiting and training young pages in good manners.

Location: _____

Speaker: chamber maid   merchant's wife   queen

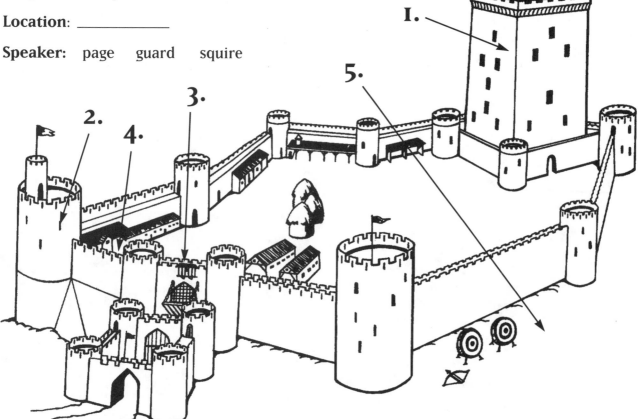

Name _____

Gargoyles, Arches, and Columns

During the late Middle Ages, people began to decorate their castles with architectural features borrowed from another important medieval building, the cathedral.

Directions

Draw a picture of each medieval architectural feature listed on this page. Try to find some of these things on famous buildings in books and magazines—or in your own neighborhood!

gargoyle

A famous gargoyle on a French cathedral sticks its tongue out at passersby!

A building I know that has a gargoyle is

_____ .

(address or name of building)

column

The Greeks and Romans invented columns long before medieval times.

A building I know that has a column is

_____ .

(address or name of building)

arch

These are used especially around windows and doorways.

A building I know that has an arch is

_____ .

(address or name of building)

tower or turret

Towers were usually round and smooth to keep invaders from climbing up.

A building I know that has a tower is

_____ .

(address or name of building)

Special Project
Make a Castle Keep, Tower, and Gatehouse

The Keep

Materials

half-gallon milk or juice carton

gray and black tempera paints

scissors

construction paper

compass (optional)

glue or tape

ruler

stapler

1. Cut off top of carton.

2. Paint carton gray. Let dry.

3. Use black paint or markers to draw in stones on all four sides of carton. Or, to replicate the look of uncut masonry, use a compass to make overlapping arcs, then trace over them with paint or marker.

4. To make crenels, mark half-inch slits from top of carton. Cut slits. Fold down every other tab. (See diagram 1)

5. Cut small rectangles of construction paper for arrow loops. Paste around top edges of keep.

The Tower

Materials

cardboard paper-towel roll

gray and black tempera paints

pencil

compass

scissors

tape or glue

toothpick

assorted construction paper for flags

1. Paint paper-towel roll gray. Let dry.

2. Use black marker or paint to draw stones or uncut masonry on roll.

3. To make roof, trace around one end of paper-towel roll. Adjust width of compass to fit circle. Now readjust so compass width is about twice the size of circle. Draw larger circle onto black construction paper and cut it out.

4. Cut slit from the edge of circle to its center. Glue the cut edges of the circle to form a cone-shaped roof. Paint roof black. (See diagram 2)

5. Repeat Steps 4 and 5 from The Keep to make crenels and arrow loops.

6. Glue roof in place on one end of paper-towel roll. Make a construction-paper flag, glue to toothpick, and poke through top of tower.

7. Attach tower to keep with tape.

THE GATEHOUSE

Materials

quart-size milk or juice carton

scissors

gray and black tempera paints

oak tag

glue

2 pieces of twine, 8 in.
(20 cm) each

1. Repeat Steps 1–4 for making keep, but use quart-size carton instead.

2. Make an arc in the middle of one wall. Use scissors to poke a hole at the top of the arc. Cut out drawbridge door, leaving bottom edge intact.

3. Pull down top of drawbridge door.

4. Make two holes of equal height in the gatehouse, next to doorway cutout.

5. Cut out a strip of oak tag the same width as the two holes in the gatehouse wall and a little longer than the drawbridge door. Punch a hole corresponding to each gatehouse hole on each side of the strip. Glue strip to back of drawbridge door. (SEE DIAGRAM 3.)

6. Lace each piece of twine through each hole in door-strip, then through corresponding hole in gatehouse. Tie a knot at each end, leaving enough slack in string so that drawbridge can be lowered and raised.

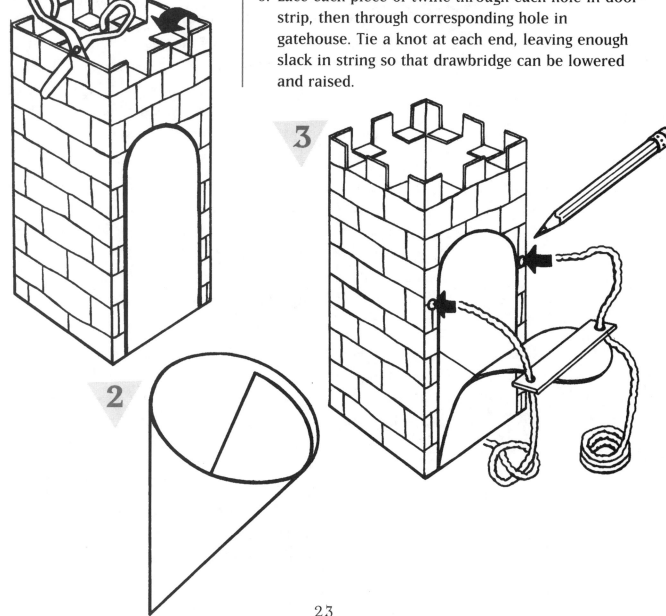

ELEANOR OF AQUITAINE

Eleanor was born in 1122 in Aquitaine, France. When Eleanor was 15, her father arranged for her to marry Prince Louis VII of France. Louis became the king of France a month after their marriage took place.

FIRST ONE MARRIAGE, THEN ANOTHER

During their marriage, Eleanor gave birth to two daughters. She also helped King Louis rule the country for 15 years. Eventually, Eleanor divorced Louis, but she did not stay single for long. In 1154, Eleanor married Henry Plantaganet, Count of Anjou, who was William the Conqueror's great-grandson. King Henry II was a short, handsome man with red hair. He was intelligent, but bad-tempered, and would scream, cry, and roll on the ground when he didn't get his way.

Two years after their marriage, Henry became King of England. Eleanor was a queen once again. Pregnant with her fourth child, Eleanor went to London with her new husband and their newborn son, William. She brought many elegant items with her, including beautiful linens, silk pillows, wine, spices, and tapestries to cover the walls. She also brought storytellers and singing poets called troubadors to entertain herself and her court.

Eleanor taught her English court about a special code of behavior called chivalry. This was a set of rules for how men and women should behave. Part of the code of chivalry was based on the concept of courtly love. A knight would promise to be a lady's obedient servant, doing almost anything to win his lady's favor. This code of conduct encouraged love between people who were not married. This may have been because, in those times, people usually did not marry for love. Their marriages were often arranged by their parents. Many people were unhappy in their marriages.

LIFE AS QUEEN OF ENGLAND

Eleanor had eight children with Henry. Besides taking care of her children, she also had to take care of the castles where her family lived. Her daily chores included making sure there would always be plenty of food, overseeing the spinners who made cloth, and helping to train pages. But Queen Eleanor was different in many ways from other medieval queens because she also helped her husband make important political decisions. She even traveled with Henry on holy wars, or crusades, and to visit different parts of their kingdom.

Over the years, Eleanor became frustrated with Henry because he stopped listening to her advice and the advice of their sons, Richard and John. Eleanor, Richard, and John led a revolt against King Henry to force him off the throne, but it failed. King Henry was so upset with Eleanor for plotting against him that he locked her away in an abbey for 16 years. Eleanor was only released for public ceremonies and to celebrate Christmas.

After King Henry died, in 1189, his son Richard became king and immediately released his mother from prison. Eleanor then ruled England for Richard while he was on crusades. After Richard's death, her other son, John, became King of England. Eleanor also helped John rule England.

Eventually, Eleanor retired to an abbey in France, where she died at the age of 82. She was buried next to her favorite son, Richard the Lion-Hearted. Over time, Eleanor became known as the Queen Who Surpassed All Queens.

ELEANOR OF AQUITAINE

Name _____

İf You Were Queen Eleanor

Use some of the vocabulary words at the bottom of this page to answer these questions.

1. On the back of this paper, write a letter to a friend in France describing your new husband, King Henry.

2. Explain to one of your ladies-in-waiting what courtly love is and why it is useful.

   _____

   _____

3. King Henry has found out about your plot against him. What is the first thing you will say to him when he asks you about it?

   _____

   _____

4. King Henry has told you of his plans to lock you in the abbey. Explain how this feels and why you think it is fair or unfair.

   _____

   _____

   _____

5. During the 16 years you are imprisoned in the abbey, what things do you do to stay busy?

   _____

   _____

Vocabulary

quarrels	discontent	abbey
oversee	troubadors	chivalry
linen	ceremony	conduct
station	feast	plot
tapestries	revolt	courtly

Girls & Women
in the Middle Ages

Women in the Middle Ages had few rights and many responsibilities. In those days, boys were thought to be stronger than girls. Because physical work was important, people often valued sons over daughters. But women and girls were extremely important to everyday life. They performed tasks, such as preparing meals and making cloth, that made it possible for families to survive.

The main job of most medieval women, whether rich or poor, was to take care of their homes and families. A young girl spent most of her day helping her mother in the house so that she could learn to care for her own home when she grew up.

Noblewomen, Townswomen, & Peasant Women

The jobs of a typical noblewoman included directing the people who ran the staff of her manor house; entertaining important visitors; keeping track of how money was spent; and stocking provisions such as cloth, wool, and food. Some noblewomen also had the job of making sure the manor could be defended during wars.

Some noble daughters were taught to care for other young children so that the daughters could later be governesses, or "cradle rockers," to other noble children. The most respected cradle rockers earned money, lands, and manors from members of the royal family. When princes or princesses grew up, they often called upon their beloved governesses to raise their own children.

Townswomen also had many jobs. They cared for livestock, smoked meats, baked, made cheese and butter, and took care of their gardens. Some townswomen also ran schools, sold things they made, and watched over male and female renters. A woman living in town could buy many products, but she had to be a good bargainer, finding the best prices for everything.

Though few women were formally educated, they often had to develop good math skills to bargain well.

A peasant woman's job was so important that if she died, became ill, or was simply lazy, her family would be in serious trouble. Peasant women kept their houses clean; cooked; made cloth and clothes; cared for children; and made cheese, butter, and ale. They also helped men and boys in the fields. Peasant women grew their own herbs and vegetables and provided a large amount of the goods that were paid as taxes to the lord of the manor.

WOMEN OUTSIDE THE HOME

Most women did not have jobs outside their homes. But those who did were often nurses. This was usually a low-paying job, though nurses hired by wealthy families did a little better. One group of nursing women, called the Cellites, not only cared for the sick but were also responsible for growing medicinal herbs, making and cleaning linens used for bandages, preparing meals, and tending fires. These nurses often made house calls on the sick and dying.

Some women were bold enough to become doctors, though it was frowned upon by most people. Sometimes a woman would show such excellent skills at healing that other doctors in the town would accuse her of witchcraft and force her to move away.

Women who managed to save their money became moneychangers, lending funds to merchants and shippers. Moneychangers would charge interest, or extra fees, for the money they loaned. Though some women got rich this way, most eventually gave this profession up because it was declared illegal.

Other women became merchants and shippers. They would invest some of their money in the ship, collecting profits, or money made from the merchandise sold. Some women owned their own shipping businesses, trading wine, oils, wax, and silks.

Women living in the Middle Ages also worked as candlemakers, alemakers, and cloth merchants. Some of these women became street hawkers, selling the things they made by the side of the road. If these women made enough money, they might buy or rent shops to sell their wares.

Name _____

Design a Tapestry

Noblewomen often used their sewing skills to create tapestries. These elaborate scenes on heavy cloth told religious and romantic stories.

Directions

- Think of a fairy tale you particularly like. Write a paragraph summarizing the story.

- Divide your story into four main parts. Think of pictures and symbols that describe each scene.

- Fill in each of the tapestry panels below with one scene from the story. Remember: No words allowed!

- Trade the finished tapestry with your friends to see if they can guess what story you are telling. Is it hard to tell a story in pictures only? Why or why not?

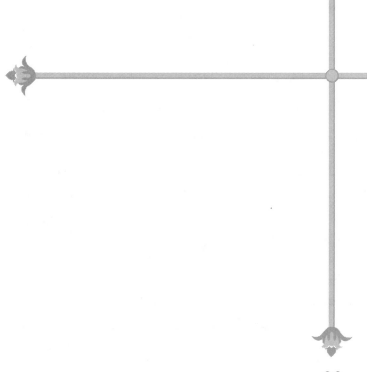

Name _____

Do Someone a Favor

According to the rules of courtly love, people showed admiration for one another by exchanging personal belongings such as ribbons or scarves. Some nobles decorated their favors with their own coats of arms. People wore these favors on their belts.

Directions

- Think of three people you admire. Write one name on each favor below.

- On each favor, write why you admire the person.

- Decorate each favor with the coat-of-arms you made in Chapter 1.

- Give each person you admire a favor. (Why not do them a favor, while you're at it?)

This favor is for _____.

I admire you because _____

_____.

From: _____

This favor is for _____.

I admire you because _____

_____.

From: _____

This favor is for _____.

I admire you because _____

_____.

From: _____

Medieval Clothing

By the time Eleanor of Aquitaine was born, medieval clothing had become much more stylish—at least for rich people. But during the early Middle Ages, people were too busy fighting battles and trying to survive to give much thought to their clothes. They were concerned mostly with keeping warm and dry.

Early Styles

Most clothing in the early Middle Ages was made of sheep's wool. Though wool can be heavy and scratchy, it also dries quickly and lasts a long time. People also layered garments to stay comfortable. The first layer of clothing was usually a T-shaped undertunic with very long sleeves. If their hands got cold, people just pulled their sleeves down to warm them.

The woman's undertunic was full-length, covered by a shorter T-shaped tunic that might be lined with fur and embroidered with beautiful stitching. Men wore knee-length tunics over woolen braccae (breeches). These baggy pants were held snugly to the legs with leather straps that crisscrossed each lower leg.

Except for soldiers, who wore helmets in battle, most men in the early Middle Ages went without caps. They grew their hair at least to their shoulders and kept beards long to keep their faces warm. They would part these beards down the middle and braid the sections into long points.

Girls and unmarried women wore their hair long or plaited into beautiful braids. Married women wore hooded cloaks called head rails. Head rails were long pieces of fabric—long enough to cover the back but short in the front to show the face. These head rails were held on by chaplets made of thin metal strips that looked like small crowns. Chaplets were sometimes decorated with flowers or jewels.

Instead of coats, most medieval people wore mantles. Mantles were capes clasped at the shoulder with pins called brooches. Shoes were usually thick oval-shaped pieces of leather wrapped around the foot with flat leather strips.

People who lived in what is now France wore slightly different styles than other Europeans. Tunics were slit up the sides and back for easier horseback riding. Women's tunics were very full and long, sweeping all the way to the floor. The sleeves of outer tunics were so wide that they often reached to the floor, too. These tunics were loosely belted at the waist. Women's veils were so long that they could be used as capes.

The Later Middle Ages

From 1000 to 1200, men's tunics became looser, sometimes reaching all the way to the floor. Women's undertunics were now made of a light fabric called cotton gauze. Overtunics were cut with low V-necks in front. Over these tunics, women wore corsets fastened tightly around their waists. Belts were draped loosely around the hips below the corset. Both men and women wore shorter outer tunics called houppelandes, which had fringes on the edges and huge sleeves.

East Asian Styles

As merchants and crusaders traveled to and from east Asia, they brought foreign styles back to Europe. Women's headpieces became more elaborate. Noblewomen wore barbettes, caps with nets that held their hair in place. They also wore scarves that wrapped around the head and throat. Another hat style was the coif, which was shaped like a box and hung with a wimple, a piece of material that could be wound around the neck.

Shoe styles also changed in the later Middle Ages. Tall platform soles were attached to the feet with straps. Leather shoes were still popular, but the toes were now formed into long points. Some of these pointed shoes, called poulaines, curled all the way to the knee, making it very difficult to walk.

By the 1400s, women were wearing sideless dresses over long-sleeved tunics. These dresses had enormous armholes from shoulder to hip. Men's tunics were now shorter and had wider, embroidered hems. Woolen breeches were replaced with tight hose of various colors. Over these tunics, men wore hooded shoulder capes. Eventually these tunics came to look like the men's shirts we see today.

Noble Fashions

This nobleman and his wife lived in 1350.
Use the key below to color each figure's outfit.

Color her mantle YELLOW.

Color her brooch RED.

Color her coif BLUE.

Add a RED tunic.

Color his hose BROWN.

Color his houppelande BLUE.

Color his shoes RED.

Name _____

WEAVE A TABLON

Wealthy medieval people wore woven patches called tablons on their clothing. A unicorn tablon was thought to bring good luck in marriage. A dog stood for love of home. A lion meant the wearer was strong and loyal.

Materials

oak tag

colorful yarn

ruler

scissors

tape

To make a Weaving Card Loom

1. Cut out the picture of the lion on this page. Trace it onto oak tag. Retrace the lines, too.

2. Cut a small slit at the top and bottom of each line. These lines will make the warp of your loom.

3. Starting at the top of the first line on the left, wrap colorful yarn up and down the card. (Don't worry about the crisscrosses you make on the back.) Tape yarn ends to the back of your card.

To Weave the Weft of the Tablon

1. Cut pieces of yarn a little longer than the widest part of the card.

2. Tape one end of each piece of yarn to the back of your card to hold it in place.

3. Weave strands of yarn under and over each warp string. Tape ends of yarn to the back of the card. Continue until your card is covered with weaving.

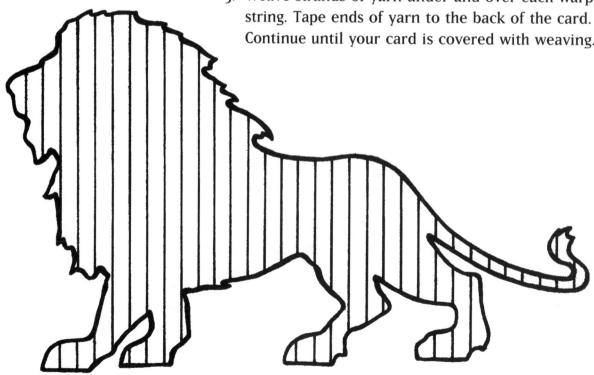

T̶H̶E̶ Feast

During the Middle Ages, feasts were given to honor visiting royalty or knights returning from battle. Feasting also took place during royal weddings or coronations, Christmas and Easter, and on saints' birthdays. Some feasts began at nine o'clock in the morning and continued for 24 hours!

Queen of the Feast

The queen or lady of the manor was usually in charge of feasts. She planned all the supplies needed for a good meal and arranged for entertainment between courses, such as dancing and singing.

Feasting usually took place within the great hall, which served as a very large dining room. The high table, where royalty and important people sat, was usually set on a raised platform. The people sitting at this table had their own servants attend them during the meal and were guarded by food tasters who would sample each bite of food to make sure it was not poisoned.

Other feasters, such as knights, their wives, squires, and ladies-in-waiting, sat at tables around the edges of the hall. These people were waited on by the knights' and squires' pages. Dogs crouched around the tables waiting for the scraps that people threw on the floor. (Bones and leftovers that were not eaten by the dogs sometimes rotted on the floor for months!)

The queen controlled what, when, and how the feast's food was made and served. She also had to be careful to respect the customs of important guests from different countries. For that reason, few medieval feasts were exactly the same.

Medieval Menu

The first course of a feast might include different kinds of cheeses, pickles, carrots, olives, grapes, melons, berries, and bread. Soups and stews came next as the second course. Chicken soup was quite popular in the Middle Ages and, like other liquid dishes, was often served in "trenchers," or bowls that were sometimes carved out of bread. After the feasters had eaten their soup, the trenchers were collected for the poor.

The third course was usually some sort of stuffed meat such as beef, pork, or lamb. To prepare meat for roasting, it would be gutted, cleaned, and speared on an iron bar. Then it would be hung over an open fire and cooked for many hours. Fish might be roasted or boiled. Fowl such as chicken, duck, capon, pheasant, and other wild birds was also served.

Sometimes, after plucking and cooking a swan or peacock, a cook might glue its beautiful feathers back onto its body before serving!

The fourth course of a feast consisted of desserts. Ingredients we often use today to make sweets, such as chocolate and sugar, were not available in the Middle Ages. Cooks used a combination of flour, fruit, honey, butter, milk or cream, and nuts and spices to make desserts that might taste unexciting but looked quite interesting. A sweet almond paste called marzipan was often molded into the shapes of fruits or animals.

The final course was some sort of salad to help digest all the rich food. Salad was made of green leafy vegetables dribbled with a dressing of oil, vinegar, and herbs or with fruit juice.

Name _____

Planning a Feast

Few noblewomen, including queens, knew how to read and write. But they did know how to cipher, or calculate, ingredients for the huge feasts they planned.

Directions

Try some of these medieval math problems to calculate the provisions needed to feed 100 people.

The First Course

1. Each guest will be given half a pound of yellow cheese. How many pounds of cheese must be bought? _____

2. If each wheel of cheese weighs 20 pounds, how many wheels will be needed altogether?

_____

3. Pickles come in a 30-gallon barrel. If each barrel contains about 20 pickles per gallon, how many pickles are in one barrel? _____

The Second Course

4. Each trencher can hold about 1/4 pound of stew. How many pounds of stew should be made? _____

5. One turnip is needed for each trencher. If each turnip weighs 1/5 pound, how many pounds are going to be needed? _____

The Third Course

6. If every two people shared a roasted chicken and each chicken needs 2 cups of stuffing, how much stuffing will feed all your guests? _____

✦ 7. One stuffed chicken weighs 3 pounds. Each chicken must be cooked for 30 minutes per pound. If you can cook 10 chickens at one time, how long will it take to cook 50 chickens?

_____

✦ Extra challenging

Name _____

Crown Thyself!

Use the designs on this page, or those you find in other books, to create a crown to wear at a feast or other medieval celebration.

Materials (for one crown)

oak tag, 11 by 15 in. (28 by 38 cm)

tape measure

2 c papier-mâché

20 newspaper strips, each approximately 6 in. (15 cm) long

gold and silver paints

1 c hard candy: green, blue, red, purple

pasta shapes (wheels, diamonds, animals), painted gold and silver

glue

To Make the Crown

1. Ask a friend to measure around your head with the tape measure. Add an extra inch to the measurement.

2. Position your oak tag lengthwise. Make a mark 5 inches from the bottom of the paper. This will give you a good idea of how high your crown should be when you draw your design.

3. Choose one of the basic crown designs on this page to copy onto oak tag. Or use a design from another book about the Middle Ages.

4. Cut around your design.

5. Fit the crown around your head. Ask a friend to help you tape the ends together. Remove the crown and staple for extra hold.

To Decorate

1. Soak newspaper strips in papier-mâché. Wrap strips around crown until it is the thickness you want.

2. After papier-mâché has dried, decorate crown with gold and silver paint.

3. When paint has dried, glue on hard candy "jewels" and pasta shapes.

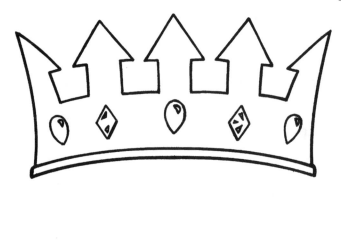

SPECIAL PROJECT: RECIPES
MEAD, TRENCHERS, AND JEWELS OF THE EAST

Try some of these recipes to make your own medieval minifeast.

MEAD

Ingredients

2 qts water

1 c honey

dried fruit (apples, apricots, raisins)

allspice

Combine water with honey in large pitcher. Stir in fruit pieces and allspice (to taste). Let sit overnight. Stir again and serve.

STEW TRENCHERS

Ingredients (per serving)

1/4 lb (113.5 gr) stew meat, cut into 1-inch cubes

turnips, washed and cut into bite-size pieces

chopped onions (optional)

1 c (220 g) carrots, peeled and diced

1/2 c (125 g) celery, washed and diced

1/4 c (60 g) string beans

1/4 c (60 g) peas

seasonings to taste (salt, pepper, savory, thyme)

8 T (125 g) cornstarch

1 c (220 g) cold water (for one crock pot full of stew)

cooking oil

sandwich roll

To Make Stew

1. Brown stew meat in oil.

2. Place stew and seasonings in boiling water. Simmer.

3. After about 90 minutes, stir in turnips and carrots.

4. Continue cooking until meat is fork tender.

5. Add celery and peas to stew mixture; cook half an hour longer.

6. Mix cornstarch with cold water until well blended.

7. Slowly pour cornstarch mixture into stew, stirring constantly, until thickened.

Stew Trenchers

continued

To Make Trenchers

1. Cut off the top of the roll as you would a jack-o'-lantern. Save "lid."

2. Dig out the inside of the loaf.

3. Fill trencher with stew. Set the bread "lid" back onto the trencher.

Jewels of the East

Ingredients

pitted dates

1/2 t peanut butter

confectioner's sugar

1. Insert scissors into one end of a date; cut the date in half lengthwise.

2. Scrape out some of the date meat. Fill fruit with peanut butter. Using a small amount of water, pinch the edges of the date together.

3. Roll date in powdered sugar.

Joan of Arc

Joan of Arc was born in Domremy-la-Pucell, France, in about 1421. As a peasant, Joan could neither read nor write. She spent most of her time herding sheep and cattle. During harvest time, she also worked in the fields.

Joan lived during a dangerous time. For about 100 years, the English and French had been fighting over the same lands. Now the English controlled many regions of France.

Visions and Voices

Like most people of the Middle Ages, Joan was very religious. When she was about 13 years old, Joan began to see visions of angels. She believed they spoke to her, telling her to be good, obey her parents, and pray often.

One day, Joan claimed that Saint Margaret and Saint Catherine had ordered her on a mission from God. According to Joan, she was to bring Charles, the dauphin prince of France, to Reims, where French kings had been crowned for 1,000 years. This would return the throne to the French. It would also mean fighting against the English army who occupied Reims and many of its surrounding lands.

Joan's message attracted the attention of many important people. They were able to get Joan a horse and a suit of boy's clothing for the long ride to Bourges, where the dauphin lived. Joan dressed as a boy because a girl traveling alone would have attracted too much attention.

When Joan arrived at the dauphin's court, priests questioned her for over three weeks. Finally they decided that Joan might indeed be able to free them from the English. Charles gave Joan a suit of white armor, a horse, and a banner sewn with religious symbols to protect her from harm. The dauphin and his soldiers, including Joan, were ready to march into battle.

Joan Becomes a Warrior

Joan knew nothing about war, but even after she was wounded, she continued to battle the English. The other soldiers felt honored to fight alongside her. Finally, with Joan's careful planning, the French army was able to drive away the English and enter Reims. Joan stood beside Charles as he was crowned on July 16, 1429.

But the French did not stop there. They wanted to be completely free of the English. So Joan and her fellow soldiers continued to fight. Joan was wounded two more times, then was captured by the English in 1430. After her capture the English placed Joan on trial for witchcraft and heresy, or crimes against the Church.

English priests said that only churchmen, not peasants, could communicate with God.

Joan was told that if she confessed to lying about her visions, she would receive a sentence of life in prison instead of death. The English questioned her every day for ten weeks. Not once did King Charles VII try to help Joan.

All of this was more than Joan could stand. Tired, weak, and confused, Joan signed a confession stating that she had lied about the voices and visions. The next day, Joan decided she did not want to confess after all. She believed in what she had done. She took back her confession and was immediately sentenced to death. On May 30, 1431, Joan was burned to death in the marketplace of Rouen. As she was dying, an English soldier shouted, "We have burned a saint!"

Five hundred years later, the Catholic Church did declare Joan a saint.

Joan of Arc

Name _____

If You Were Joan of Arc

Use some of the vocabulary words on the bottom of this page to answer these questions.

1. What would you say to people who told you that the voices you heard were unreal?

    _____

    _____

    _____

2. On the back of this paper, write a short letter to a friend explaining what the voices of Saint Catherine and Saint Margaret have ordered you to do.

3. What might you say to Charles to convince him to go to Reims with you?

    _____

    _____

4. During your trial, priests tell you that only special churchmen can talk to God. What would you say to this?

    _____

    _____

5. You are a descendant of Joan of Arc. You want the Catholic Church to declare Joan a saint. How would you convince the pope that he should do this?

    _____

    _____

    _____

Vocabulary

confession	inspiration	trial	sorcery	hallucinations
pray	imprisonment	exhaustion	inquisitor	visions
cathedral	saints	committee	dauphin	heresy

Peasant Life

Joan of Arc was the daughter of a wealthy peasant. Her father owned land and, unlike serfs and other peasants, was able to sell his crops for money. This happened more often near the end of the Middle Ages, but it was still unusual during Joan's time.

The Life of a Serf

In the beginning of the Middle Ages, more than half of all people living in France, England, and Germany were serfs. They owned very little and spent most of their time working.

The lord and lady of the manor allowed serfs to live in "wattle-and-daub" cottages made of mud and straw. Each serf was given a small piece of land for growing vegetables and raising livestock. In return the serfs owed rent and taxes to the lord. Since they usually had very little money, serfs paid these fees in labor and crops.

Each manor's farm land was divided into three parts. Each year two of the fields were split up into strips to be planted, while the third field remained unplanted, or fallow. A serf might be granted one part of one strip to farm. Other parts belonged to the lord and lady of the manor, and the rest belonged to the church.

The serfs worked on their lord's lands for three days and their own lands for the next three days. The work day was from sunup to sundown. For dinner, peasants ate simple meals of vegetables, bread, and ale. On special occasions they might enjoy some rabbit or pork. Children drank boiled water or watered-down beer. Serfs rested from farming every Sunday and on holy days.

Serfs led difficult lives. Their lords could beat or starve them without good reason. Their land might be rocky and hard to farm. Serfs' cottages were often windowless shacks with dirt floors. The air inside was smoky because most homes did not have chimneys. During the winter, animals such as sheep and cows lived in a little shed just outside the door of the cottage, making it even smellier inside than usual. The straw beds on which most peasants slept were usually filthy and filled with bugs.

If a serf wanted to leave his lord's manor, he had to run away and remain free from capture for one year and one day. However, if he was captured within that one year and a day, he was returned to his lord's manor and harshly punished.

From Serfs to Peasants

As money and trade grew throughout Europe, some serfs were able to run away and build new villages on the eastern frontiers of Germany and France. They learned how to trade what they grew for real wages. Some became craftsmen and even merchants. Because there were fewer people left to work as farmers for the nobility, the remaining peasants were able to bargain for wages and lower rents.

Eventually most serfs became small farmers or peasants. Even so, their lives were filled with hardship. A favorite story among peasants was called *The Vision of Piers Plowman* by William Langland. It is a sad tale about a farmer who was treated unfairly by the landowners. The story expresses the anger that peasants felt toward wealthy lords and kings who spent their hard-earned taxes on feasts, fancy clothes, and silly wars.

Peasant Tasks

It is not hard to see why peasants were often miserable. Their lives were filled with hard work. Even the smallest peasant children worked, digging the rocks out of the garden, collecting eggs, raising rabbits, and caring for younger brothers and sisters. At around the age of 14, some peasant children became shepherds, guarding their lords' sheep from wild animals. When spring came, shepherds were usually responsible for shearing or cutting the wool off the sheep. This wool would be spun into threads, which were then turned into material for clothing.

Most of this material was given to the nobles of the castle. Each year, luckier peasants might be given enough leftover material to make one new outfit for each family member.

Life for peasants became easier over time, especially as new laws were written that gave them the same rights as other people. Better schools and education systems also opened up other opportunities for farmers and peasants.

The Herbal Healer

There were few trained doctors in the Middle Ages. Peasants grew herbs in backyard gardens to treat diseases and other misfortunes and to grant special powers.

Directions

Use the herbal glossary at the bottom of the page to write a prescription (Rx) for each ailment or condition.

1) Mistress Fishwife complains that her pantry is full of weevils. She has also not recovered her strength from the birth of her seventh child.

Rx

2) John the Miller says he cannot stop crying over the death of his young wife and has trouble sleeping.

Rx

3) Gyslaine the Cooper's daughter is nearly 18 years old and wants a husband. (All of her other friends have been married for years.)

Rx

4) William the Plowman has been kicked by his horse. He also must appear before the lord of the manor tomorrow and is nervous.

Rx

5) The family of Rachel of Ashton is sick with a chest cold.

Rx

Ailments and Conditions	Herbs
Grief	Sage
Lovableness	Thyme
Insects	Lavender
Courage	Borage
Swelling and bruising	Marjoram
Coughing and spewing	Lungwort
Weakness	Rosemary
Nightmares and insomnia	Chamomile

A

EVERYDAY ARTIFACTS

Peasants and serfs owned very few personal belongings. Most of the items they did own were important to their everyday work.

DIRECTIONS

Use the names in the artifacts box at the bottom of the page to label each picture. Describe how you think each item was used.

A)

What is it? _____

How was it used? _____

_____

B)

What is it? _____

How was it used? _____

_____

C)

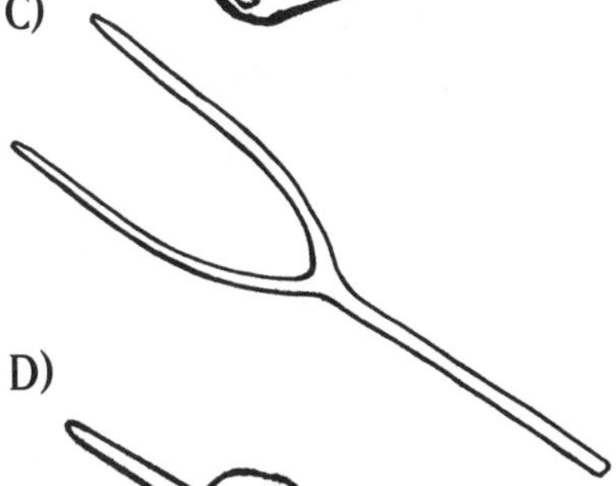

What is it? _____

How was it used? _____

_____

D)

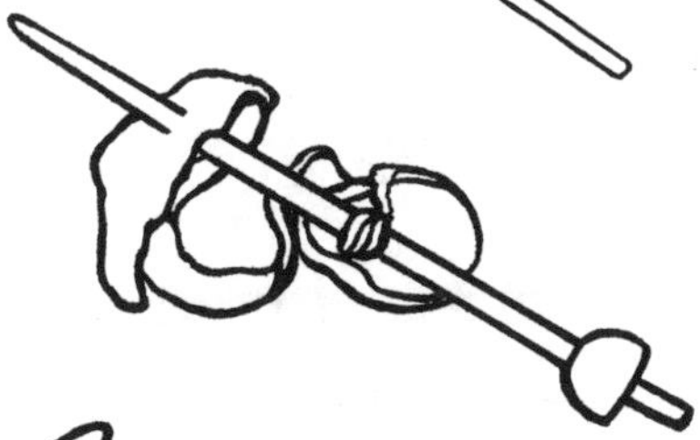

What is it? _____

How was it used? _____

_____

E)

What is it? _____

How was it used? _____

_____

Artifact Names

billhook	spindle	flesh-hook
costrel, or flask	pitchfork	

THE CHURCH

Joan of Arc was not unusual in her deeply held religious beliefs. Bloody wars and terrible diseases were a fact of life for everyone in the Middle Ages. People died of everything from childbirth to pig bites to falling into pots of boiling water. Few people lived past the age of 30. Because their lives were hard, people prayed to find comfort and looked forward to a better life after death.

But religion was important in the Middle Ages for another reason. It brought law and order to a difficult time. The most powerful religious organization in Europe at this time was the Roman Catholic Church. The Church held and maintained many lands. It developed and used its own money system, and had its own court system and laws.

HOW THE CHURCH WAS ORGANIZED

The most powerful person in the Catholic Church was the pope. Throughout most of the Middle Ages, he ruled over all the clergy, or Church officials, from Rome, Italy.

A pope was chosen from a group of Church rulers called cardinals. Serving under the cardinals were the archbishops. The archbishops were very much like dukes or barons. They held large churches and lands much as a knight would hold a fief.

Archbishops often decided when and where a cathedral, or large church, would be built. To raise money to build a cathedral, which could take 50 years to complete, the archbishop would ask the pope and other Church officials for help. Church leaders would also collect money and taxes from peasants and nobles for the new cathedral.

Building these great cathedrals gave local masons, carpenters, and artisans work, food, and a place to live. But this work was also dangerous. Builders used new technologies, or ideas, some of which may not have been tested before. Sometimes a part of the church would collapse, and workers would be killed.

Bishops and Priests

Bishops controlled the local monasteries and lands and were often advisors to kings and noblemen. Some bishops and archbishops even had their own armies of soldiers that they could loan to the nobles for wars.

Finally, there were the priests. Some lived in villages, where they performed religious services for villagers and peasants. Another type of priest, called friars, traveled from village to village, often preaching outdoors.

The final group of priests, called monks, lived in special places called monasteries. They spent their time studying, praying, and sometimes helping the poor. Monks grew their own food and made clothing and wine. In the days before the printing press, monks also copied valuable books. They decorated these books with beautiful designs and borders. Because of their hard work, we can read ancient stories that might otherwise have been lost long ago.

Religion in Everyday Life

Priests, monks, and other Church officials were a part of the everyday lives of everyone in the Middle Ages. Almost every nobleman hired one or more priests as members of his household staff. These clerics would conduct a special mass, or church service, each day. Because few noblemen could write, the staff priests would write important letters and documents. They would also give advice about wars, laws, family quarrels, and the education and marriage of noble sons and daughters.

For the peasants the local churches provided the same services as today's hospitals, hotels, and schools. During saints' days, priests provided food and drink to the hungry peasants. Priests rang church bells that told everyone the time of day. This was especially important during a time when there were few clocks and no wristwatches. People also relied on the church to protect them if they were accused of breaking a law.

But sometimes the Church itself made unfair laws. For instance, a husband might be allowed to beat his wife without being punished. People could be accused of witchcraft and punished by members of the Church. The Church taught that poor people should accept their condition and not try to change it. The Church made a law forbidding women to serve as priests, though women were allowed to become nuns, helping the community and teaching other women.

Name _____

Quills and Ink

Quills

Materials

large feathers from your backyard or a craft store

sharp scissors (Ask an adult for permission!)

1. Cut or peel off part of the feather so that you can hold the quill more easily while writing.

2. Carefully cut the end of the feather at an angle.

3. Make a small slit up the side of the quill. This will help the quill hold ink so that you don't need to redip it as often.

4. Snip the end of your quill as you use it to keep it sharp.

Ink

Materials

(to make one cup of ink)

1 T sugar

1 c warm water

1 c of one type of the following berries:
cherries for red
blueberries for blue
raspberries for burgundy
blackberries for purple

2 clean glass jars

glass bowl

coffee filter or fine-mesh strainer

potato masher

funnel

1. Dissolve sugar in warm water.

2. Place washed berries in bowl. Use a potato masher to crush berries into a fine pulp.

3. Moisten the coffee filter. Use it or the strainer to strain berry juice into one of the jars.

4. Throw away the pulp and seeds. If there is any remaining pulp in the juice, pour it through the strainer or a new coffee filter again.

5. Pour small amounts of berry juice into the sugar water to make the shade you want. Use a funnel to pour your ink into the other jar.

Name _____

LETTERS TO ILLUMINATE

Use the ink and quill you made to color these letters. At the bottom of the page, make up your own illuminated letter.

THE CRUSADES

During the Middle Ages many Christians thought that people who did not believe in Christ were bad. These Christians called their religion "the one true faith."

But there were many non-Christians living outside of Europe at that time. They had held other beliefs for thousands of years. Some of these non-Christians were the Arab Muslims and Seljuk Turks who occupied the Middle East and northern Africa. Jewish people also lived in the region.

Muslims felt as strongly about their Islamic prophet, Muhammad, as Christians did about Christ. Muslims had lived in the city of Jerusalem for more than four hundred years. The religion they practiced is called Islam. Jews had their own prophet, Abraham. Jews had lived in and around Jerusalem for thousands of years. The Jewish religion is called Judaism.

The Turks occupied other parts of the region where Christ had lived, taught, and died. They had lost the capital of their empire, Constantinople, to the Christians many years earlier. Christians called this entire region the Holy Land.

REASONS FOR THE CRUSADES

The word *crusade* comes from a Latin word meaning "marked with a cross." The pope wanted his people to take part in crusades to get back the Holy Land and to change Turks, Muslims, and Jews into Christians. The pope and other Church leaders also wanted to take the many lands and riches found in the Middle East.

The leader of the Catholic Church, Pope Urban II, declared the first crusade in 1096. The first army of crusaders was made up of French peasants and serfs. These soldiers, who had almost no fighting experience, were eager to go on a crusade because it would mean escaping their miserable lives for a while. Their leaders, Peter the Hermit and Walter the Penniless, promised them riches for their efforts. The peasant crusaders caused much damage during their march to the Holy Land. When they finally arrived in Nicaea, Turkey, the Turkish army massacred nearly all of these Christian soldiers.

The next group of crusaders traveled to Constantinople in 1097. This group included knights who had brought along their families and servants. Altogether, about 30,000 people traveled into Asia Minor to attack the Turks. By the time they reached Jerusalem, more than half of the crusaders had died from lack of food and water. Still, they managed to capture Jerusalem in what was one of the bloodiest battles of the crusades.

THE CHRISTIANS RULE JERUSALEM

After several crusades the Christians took over Jerusalem as if they had always lived there. Many non-Christian people living in this region were killed, converted, or forced to move. Others lost their property and money to the Catholic Church. Still others were horribly tortured if they did not convert to Christianity. Great Muslim, Turkish, and Jewish works of art and literature were destroyed by the crusaders. All the while, the armies of these peoples continued to fight against the Christian invaders.

Finally, in 1187 the great Muslim leader Saladin led his army to recapture Jerusalem. King Richard the Lion-Hearted knew he could not win against Saladin, so he offered a peace treaty. The treaty allowed European pilgrims to safely visit the Holy Land. Over time many trade routes opened up between the Middle East and western Europe.

In spite of this agreement, Christians from Europe continued fighting the Muslims for about 30 years. One famous holy war was called the Children's Crusade. It was led by two boy preachers who gathered a group of children, most under the age of 12, to march to the Holy Land. Many children were sent home before they got very far, but those who reached Genoa were either killed or sold into slavery.

By the end of the thirteenth century, the Holy Land was in the hands of the Muslims once again.

Name _____

STAINED-GLASS JIGSAW

The colorful stained-glass windows of medieval churches often showed crusaders and religious saints. But, at a time when few people could read, these windows also told stories that entertained and taught lessons.

DIRECTIONS

· Cut out the pieces of stained glass below. Put them together to form a scene, or picture.

· Look at the scene carefully. What does it show? What lesson might it teach?

The lesson this stained-glass scene teaches might be _____

_____

_____

Name _____

TREASURES OF THE MUSLIM WORLD

The crusaders borrowed many inventions and ideas from the Moslems of the Middle East, who were known as brilliant scientists, artists, and traders.

DIRECTIONS

Match the names of Muslim inventions or ideas in Column I with their descriptions in Column II. Use a dictionary for extra help!

Column I	Column II
A) the astrolabe	1) a kind of mathematics
B) enamelware	2) drugstores
C) the lute	3) our counting system
D) algebra	4) a navigation instrument used by Columbus and other explorers
E) Arabian numerals	5) a musical instrument that sounds like a harp
F) apothecaries	6) a type of dish decorated with a glassy material
	7) a musical instrument you play with your mouth

SPECIAL PROJECT
TELLING-TIME CANDLES

Candles were too expensive for most people during the Middle Ages. But monks and other church officials made and used candles both to give light and tell time.

Materials (for about 40 candles)

4 lbs (1.81 kg) paraffin wax

hammer

screwdriver or chisel

5 soup cans, 32-oz (907 g) each

large cooking pot

hot plate

water

crayons and scented oil (optional)

40 segments of string, 12 in. each

pencils

large metal paper clips

ruler

black marker

plate or candleholder

timer

clean stirring stick

newspaper

(NOTE: This project requires the use of a hot plate and hot wax. Please exercise caution.)

To Prepare Drying Rack

1. Move two desks of equal height side-by-side, leaving a space slightly shorter than a pencil length.

2. Spread newspaper under desks.

To Prepare Wax

1. Use the hammer and screwdriver to break the slab of wax into chunks. Pack each soup can with wax chunks.

2. Fill large cooking pot with about 3 inches of water. Place over medium heat.

3. Carefully set several cans of wax into the warm water.

4. (Optional) If you want colored or scented candles, add peeled crayons or scented oil now.

5. Once wax has melted, turn heat to low. Do not allow wax to cool completely, as it will harden.

To Dip Candles

1. Have students use markers to write their names on pencils. Tie one end of each piece of string to the middle of a pencil; tie the other end to a paper clip.

2. Measure the string from the paper-clip end; mark 8 inches (20 cm) with a black marker. This will leave a 4-inch (10 cm) wick.

3. Dip string into wax to the 8-inch mark. After several seconds, remove string from wax. Wait several seconds, then gently and carefully pull the paper clip downward to straighten the wick.

4. Hang up wax-coated wicks by balancing the pencils between two desks.

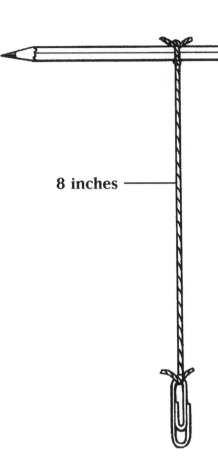

8 inches

To Finish Candles

1. After first layer of wax has dried, dip candles again. You may need to reheat wax in cans to soften it. Continue dipping until candles are desired thickness. (Note: All candles should be of approximately equal size for the following activity.)

To Make Candle "Clocks"

1. Melt some wax on a plate; stand one candle in wax until it hardens.

2. At the beginning of the hour, light the candle. Set timer for one hour. After time elapses, extinguish the flame. (If using smaller candles, measure in 15-minute increments.)

3. Compare burned candle to an unburned one. Measure the one-hour mark and mark the unburned candle accordingly. Continue measuring and making marks, using the number of marks to show how many hours have passed (for instance, two hours would be noted with two lines). You could also use more than one candle to total one hour.

4. Keep time this way for one day. Compare the marked candles with clock time. Ask students to draw conclusions about the problems of keeping track of time this way.

GEOFFREY CHAUCER

GEOFFREY CHAUCER IS THOUGHT TO BE THE GREATEST STORYTELLER OF THE MIDDLE AGES. THE DIALECT, OR STYLE, OF ENGLISH THAT HE USED IN HIS POEMS AND STORIES BECAME THE MOST POPULAR STYLE AMONG WRITERS OF THAT TIME. THE WAY CHAUCER USED THE LANGUAGE AFFECTS THE WAY WE SPEAK AND WRITE EVEN TODAY.

A POET GROWS UP

Geoffrey Chaucer was born around 1340. He probably grew up like most boys of the Middle Ages, playing in the fields, leaping, dancing, wrestling, and throwing stones. When winter came, he may have played on the frozen ponds and marshes surrounding London.

When Chaucer became an adult, he married Philippa, a well-to-do noblewoman. Chaucer soon became a favorite of the royal English court. Kings, queens, and nobles loved his poetry. They paid for his work in coins, food, and clothing. They also gave him a place within the castle to live.

Chaucer spent his days riding with the nobles through the forests, hunting, fishing, or falconing. He particularly enjoyed the great feasts given by the nobility. The writer also liked to play chess and a board game called hazard, in which players raced their game pieces, called pilgrims, to a saint's shrine or tomb.

Soon, Chaucer was appointed diplomat, traveling to different regions of Europe to keep peace between the king and his lords. He traveled in great style during these trips, often borrowing large sums of money from the king to meet his costs. In fact, Chaucer was such a big spender that he was often broke. On many occasions he had to ask his friends to pay the debts that he owed.

It is probably from his journeys as a diplomat that Chaucer came up with many of the ideas for his writing. Probably his most famous work was *The Canterbury Tales*, about a group of pilgrims traveling through England in 1387. The tales depict many different kinds of people, from a wealthy churchwoman to a miller to a knight. These stories are satires, poking fun at people living during this time. Though there are no portraits of Chaucer, we know something about the way he looked from a description he gives of himself in *The Canterbury Tales*: "He is in the waist well-shaped [fat] and seems elvish by his countenance."

OTHER JOBS

Chaucer did earn money for his stories, but it was not enough to pay his debts or

GEOFFREY CHAUCER

live in the style he liked. So, for about 12 years, Chaucer was the controller of the customs in London. He collected taxes from traders who came to the city. During this time, Chaucer lived in a house right on top of the London city wall. Later, he and his wife moved to Kent. He was elected as a representative to Parliament, a group of people who helped make laws.

After Chaucer's wife died, in 1387, he rented a house at Westminster Abbey, in London. When he died, he was buried in the abbey garden. Over the years, other poets and writers were buried next to Geoffrey Chaucer. This part of Westminster Abbey eventually became known as Poets' Corner. It is now a famous tourist attraction.

Name _____

İf You Were Chaucer

Use some of the vocabulary words at the bottom of this page to answer these questions.

1. Pretend you are Geoffrey Chaucer's ghost viewing life today. What people, places, or things would you want to write about?

   _____

   _____

2. Explain why you are always in debt and what you might do to make more money.

   _____

   _____

3. On the back of this paper, write a letter telling a friend why you have written *The Canterbury Tales* and what it is about.

4. Who might have been your favorite character in your own tales? Why?

   _____

   _____

5. You might have been friends with some of your pilgrim characters. Tell what might have happened to some of these people after the pilgrimage.

   _____

   _____

Vocabulary

poet	abbey	tale
debt	dialect	verse
diplomat	pilgrim	revise
representative	shrine	virtue
Parliament	intention	satire

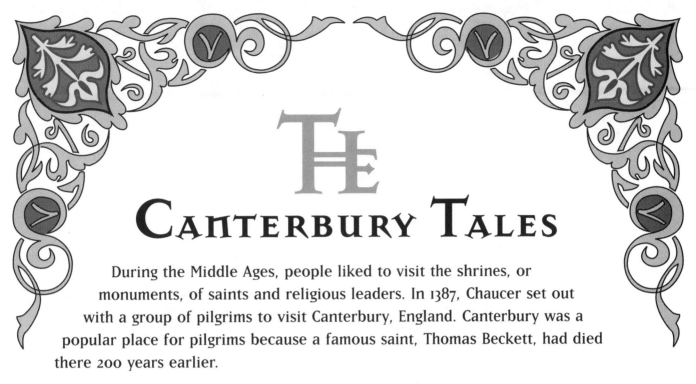

The Canterbury Tales

During the Middle Ages, people liked to visit the shrines, or monuments, of saints and religious leaders. In 1387, Chaucer set out with a group of pilgrims to visit Canterbury, England. Canterbury was a popular place for pilgrims because a famous saint, Thomas Beckett, had died there 200 years earlier.

The journey took about four days. Chaucer challenged each traveler to tell stories during the trip. After the journey, Chaucer began to revise the stories and set them to rhyme, but he died before his task was finished. These stories are not only funny, sad, and exciting, but they also have a lot to teach us about life and people in the Middle Ages.

A Summary of the Tales

Day One

The Knight is the first to tell his story. It is about two ancient princes, Palamon and Arcite, who fight against each other to win the love of Emelyne, a lovely princess. The Miller, who is drunk, then tells his story. It is so full of bad words and unpleasant scenes that Chaucer warns the sensitive reader to "turn the leaf (page)." The Reeve also tells his tale. It, too, is unpleasant and full of curses. The Cook tries to tell his tale, but is interrupted.

Day Two

The Man of Law tells about Constance, the daughter of a Roman emperor of long ago. Constance wants to marry the Sultan of Syria, but her mother becomes jealous and casts her to sea in a ship. The Prioress, a very elegant churchwoman, tells her story about a choirboy who keeps singing even after he is murdered.

The Monk tells stories about several men who have had bad luck and have lost all their money. The Priest tells the fable of Chanticleer, a rooster.

Day Three

The Doctor tells a boring story about a man who saves his daughter from a cruel judge. A few people ask the funny Pardoner to tell some jokes. Instead, after eating some cake, he tells a story about the evils of greed and gambling. Then he launches into another story about three people who die trying to get their hands on some gold. The Wife of Bath, who has had five husbands, tells a fairy tale about a knight of King Arthur's court who sets off to find out what women wish for most in life (a husband). The Summoner, who is angry at the Friar, tells a naughty story about a friar. The Friar then tells a naughty story about a summoner.

Day Four

The Squire's story is about a princess who finds a magic ring that teaches her how to speak to birds. This story is never finished. The Franklin wishes that his son was as good as this squire. He then tells a story about a woman who proves her love for a man by removing all the rocks from the coast of Brittany. A Canon and a Yeoman ride up to the group and ask if they can join. The Canon gets angry because someone insults his clothes. He rides off. But the Yeoman stays and tells a story about alchemists, or scientists who "make" gold and silver. The Cook begins to feel sick, and the Manciple accuses him of drinking too much beer. They fight and then the Manciple tells a fable about why crows are black.

THE FABLE OF CHANTICLEER

(A PLAY BASED ON A CHAUCER TALE)

> **PLAYERS**
>
> Narrator
>
> Chanticleer, a handsome rooster
>
> Pertelote, a lovely hen
>
> Sir Russell, a crafty fox
>
> A widow
>
> Some neighbors
>
> Three sows
>
> Three cows
>
> A sheep
>
> Some chickens

SCENE ONE. A BARNYARD AT NIGHT

NARRATOR: Once upon a time, there was a kindly old woman who lived in a small cottage. Her husband had died and left her just a few animals: three sows, three cows, a sheep, a yard full of chickens, and a rooster named Chanticleer. (Chanticleer, *puffing out his chest and strutting, enters with other* chickens. *The* chickens *are pecking and gossiping.*)

NARRATOR: Chanticleer had chosen one very lovely chicken, Pertelote, to be his wife. (Chanticleer *and* Pertelote *hug briefly.*)

CHANTICLEER (*stretching and yawning*): 'Tis time to hit the hay, my pretty peckers! After all, I need to be up at the break of dawn. (Chickens *cackle in agreement, and everyone goes off to their perches.* Chanticleer *and* Pertelote *fall asleep. Soon,* Chanticleer *begins to moan.*)

PERTELOTE (*shaking* Chanticleer *awake*): Chanticleer, what ails you?

CHANTICLEER: Oh, madam! I was having a very bad dream. I dreamt I was walking through our yard when a beastly dog approached me. He had horrible glowing eyes. Oooh, it was so frightening!

PERTELOTE (*shaking her claw at* Chanticleer): What? Have I married a fool! Everyone knows that bad dreams come from eating too much dinner. Now, go back to sleep!

(Chanticleer *sighs. He and* Pertelote *snuggle up together again.*)

63

SCENE 2. THE BARNYARD, NEXT MORNING

CHANTICLEER (crowing loudly): Cock-a-doodle-doo! A lovely day with skies of blue! (Flies down from his perch. Suddenly, Sir Russell sneaks into the yard. Chanticleer sees him.) Uh . . . cock-a-doodle-doo? (starts to run away)

SIR RUSSELL: Dear sir, why do you run? I have only come to hear your beautiful voice. (bows) I am Sir Russell and I have never heard such heavenly singing! (Chanticleer, pleased, stands on toes, puffs out chest, and gets ready to crow. Fox leaps up, grabs Chanticleer in his "mouth," and begins to carry him off. Sows, cows, sheep, and other chickens begin to make frightened animal noises. The Widow enters.)

WIDOW: Stop, Fox! Where are you taking my rooster? Come back this instant!

NEIGHBORS: Stop, Fox! Drop that rooster or else!

(All begin to run after Sir R. and Chanticleer, waving sticks, pitchforks, arms, and tails.)

CHANTICLEER: Sir, the crowd is closing in. If I were you, I'd tell them to turn back or risk getting lost in the forest ahead.

SIR RUSSELL: (Looks thoughtful as he considers idea. Opens his mouth to speak. Chanticleer breaks free and flies to the top of a tree.) What . . . er . . . come back here, you . . . Aaaaargh! (suddenly changes his tone) Oh, dear Chanticleer, I am so sorry to have frightened you! I only meant to take you back to sing for my forest friends. Please come back!

CHANTICLEER: No way! I was fooled once by you, but I will never trust you again! A creature will never prosper who stubbornly shuts his eyes when he should see.

FOX (looking upset): Worse luck for the creature who's so lacking in self-control that he chatters when he should keep his mouth shut! (exits)

NARRATOR: So, ladies and gentlemen, that's what happens when you let false friends fake you out with flattery. Chanticleer learned his lesson and went on to a live a happy life. Sir Russell, on the other hand, found plenty of other foolish roosters for his cooking pot.

A Medieval Education

In the early Middle Ages, the Church set up special schools that mainly taught religion. Children learned to read Latin so that they could read and copy the Bible. They learned math so that they could figure out the dates of religious holidays. They learned to sing so that they could join the church choir.

Life in a Monastery School

Monastery schools were not much fun. At around the age of seven, certain boys from wealthy families were chosen to attend. These boys were usually younger sons who were not expected to inherit the family's wealth, or boys who were not considered strong enough to become knights.

A young scholar could expect to sit long hours on a hard bench, writing on a wax tablet that could be smoothed over to correct mistakes. Children, teenagers, and adults learned the same lessons in the same classrooms. There was no recess or playtime. A boy could be beaten or even dismissed from school for merely speaking too loudly. No one was allowed to challenge ideas in the Bible, conduct experiments, or ask questions.

In the 1200s, universities were founded in some large cities. College students studied seven main topics: grammar; rhetoric (using words in clever ways); logic, or reasoning; arithmetic; geometry; music; and astronomy, the study of the stars. While this type of education was better than many monastery schools, even colleges had problems. The largest school libraries each owned fewer than 100 books. Books were so hard to find that most lessons had to be memorized or copied. In 1040 a young scholar paid for one book with 200 sheep, several bales of wheat, furs, and other goods.

Girls' Education

Before the 1200s, educating girls was considered too expensive. Noble families were expected to pay a dowry, or marriage fee, to future husbands, so they claimed they could not afford to also pay for school for their daughters. But this changed over time. People began to send girls to convent schools. Some girls studied subjects such as religion and philosophy under famous tutors at major universities.

Women who were not chosen for convent schools were sometimes tutored at home. A nobleman might pay a wandering scholar to teach his daughters prayers and Bible stories. It was rare for women to become teachers, unless you counted the many mothers who taught their own children. Some mothers borrowed and copied entire books so that their children could learn their ABCs. Women also taught their children chivalry, or manners, as well as poetry, how to read different coats of arms, dancing, and singing.

Education for Others

Eventually, schools were started for the education of merchants' children. During the 1330s, the schools of Florence, Italy, educated more than 10,000 children.

Children of the lower classes usually learned a trade or, most likely, how to farm, make home crafts, and take care of children and family.

Name _____

A Latin Lesson

Students all over Europe in the Middle Ages learned to read and write in Latin because it was the official language of the Catholic Church.

Directions

Read the clues at the bottom of this page. Find the Latin word that matches each clue. Write the word on the line.

adultus

audire

centum

curvus

libri

scribere

tempus

vox

Clues

A) Ten times ten equals _____

B) You need your ears to do this. _____

C) Libraries have many of these. _____

D) Try to keep this down while others are working. _____

E) Your teacher is one. _____

F) This sometimes flies. _____

G) You probably learned to do this in first grade. _____

H) A kind of baseball pitch, or something in the road. _____

Name _____

Ye Olde English Poetry

Before Geoffrey Chaucer most writers wrote in French or Latin. Chaucer made English a more acceptable form of expression.

Directions

The verses of English poetry on this page were written by people in Geoffrey Chaucer's day. Write the number of each poem underneath the picture you think it describes.

(1)   Bryng us in no browne bred, for that is mad of brane;

Nor bryng us in no whyt bred, for therin is no gane,

But bryng us in good ale.

(2)   He seyde to me he wolde be trewe,

And change me for non othur newe;

Now y sykke and am pale of hewe,

For he is far.

(3)   Sumer is icumen in,

Lhude sing cuccu!

Groweth sed and bloweth med

And springth the wude nu.

Sing cuccu!

Games, Sports, and Other Fun

People of the Middle Ages enjoyed having fun as much as people of today do. In fact, though they worked hard, medieval people observed more than 100 holidays or days of rest.

Performers and Fairs

Royal families often hired jugglers, acrobats, musicians, puppeteers, actors, and bards (singers) to entertain at castle feasts. As payment these entertainers would receive food, a place to sleep, and maybe even some coins. Some entertainers became so well-liked that they stayed permanently at a castle. They could be called upon at any time to perform for the king or queen.

Royal entertainers, realizing they could be fired easily, worked hard to create interesting acts. A juggler might learn to juggle axes or short swords. Actors and playwrights used wild special effects in their plays, such as dragon masks that stuck out their tongues or thin wires that made characters appear to fly. Musicians and jongleurs spent hours writing ballads that praised the deeds of the kings who employed them.

Rich people weren't the only ones who had fun. Peasants and merchants enjoyed being entertained at fairs held in villages and around castles. Besides watching performances by acrobats, jugglers, and dancing bears, fairgoers could buy cheap snacks like fried meat pies and "sweetmeats" made of marzipan. They could examine the crafts of shoemakers, cloth makers, and spinners. Fairgoers also drank a great deal of ale, or beer, at these events. Some had their fortunes told by soothsayers or marveled at holy relics, items (and even body parts) that were believed to have belonged to famous saints.

Hunting and Contests

Men and women of all classes enjoyed playing and watching sports. Bowling and tennis were popular among merchants and nobility. Members of the royal court also enjoyed hunting. They would award certain points for trapping different animals. The nobility raised falcons or sparrows to race and perform tricks. Noblewomen were especially skilled at this sport, called hawking.

Tournaments and jousts were important events for royalty and nobility. In the later Middle Ages, tournaments gave people a chance to parade before one another in fancy clothes, to flirt, and to dance. Noblemen and women even ran footraces and performed acrobatics at tournaments.

Peasants also enjoyed rough-and-tumble sports. Throwing and wrestling contests were especially popular. Some sports were especially violent. In cockfighting, people might bet on which roosters would fight one another to the death. They also challenged each other to bait, or tease, a captured bear without being attacked or killed by it.

Quieter Games

Men and women of the upper classes enjoyed playing strategy games like chess. In fact, chess was so popular that rich people had playing pieces made out of silver, ivory, and crystal. Other board games of strategy included nine-man morris, fox and geese, and hazard, a game in which players moved their game pieces around the board to reach a saint's shrine.

Nine-Man Morris ✦ (for two players)

Cut out this gameboard and read the directions below to play a game enjoyed by many people during the Middle Ages.

To Prepare

- Cut out nine round markers of one color and nine round markers of another color.

To Play

- Players must make as many mills as possible. A mill is formed when three connected circles are covered by one player's markers.

- Players take turns placing one marker at a time on any vacant circle.

- Jumping is not allowed.

- When a player makes a mill, he or she can remove one of the opponent's markers, unless it is already in a mill.

- A marker removed from the board cannot be played again.

- A mill may be "opened" by moving one of the three markers off its line during one play, then putting it back again on the next play. This forms a new mill and lets a player remove an opponent's marker from the board.

To Win

- A player must remove so many of the opponent's markers that he or she can no longer make mills or move anywhere.

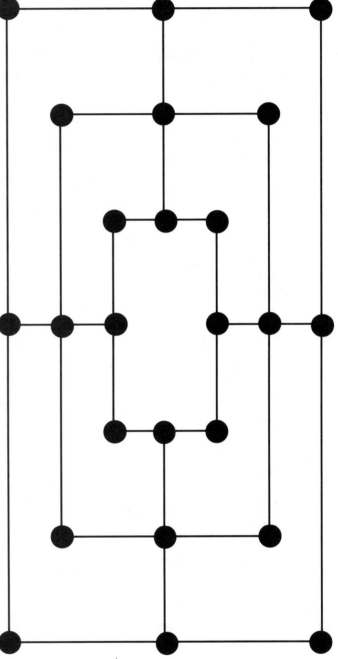

For Longer Play

- Make a rule that players are not allowed to make a mill in the same line twice in a row.

✦ NOTE TO TEACHERS: Enlarge game board for easier play.

JUGGLING BALLS

Some jugglers became quite famous for their tricks. Follow the simple directions on this page to make your own juggling balls, then practice, practice, practice!

Materials

4 felt squares in bright colors, 2.5 by 4 in. (6 by 10 cm) each

rice

small funnel

needle

strong thread

scissors

pattern from below

straight pins

1. Cut out the pattern below.

2. Pin pattern onto a piece of fabric. Cut it out. Repeat until you have cut out four pieces of fabric.

3. Cut out interesting decorations (stars, moons, squiggles) from leftover felt. Glue decorations to one side of each piece of fabric.

4. Pin two pieces of fabric together along *one* edge, decorated sides facing in, and sew together.

5. Continue this process, adding another fabric piece each time.

6. Leave a small opening in the final seam. Turn ball covering inside-out.

7. Place the small end of a funnel into the opening. Pour rice into funnel to fill up the ball.

8. Tuck edges of open seam inside ball covering and finish sewing.

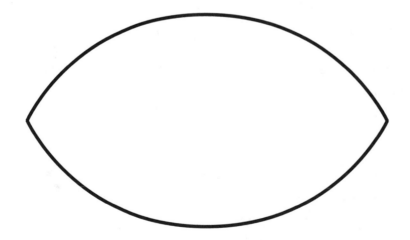

SPECIAL PROJECT

LUTES, DRUMS, AND DANCING BELLS

Use these instruments during a classroom medieval feast to accompany medieval recordings or to add a special touch to a medieval puppet show or play.

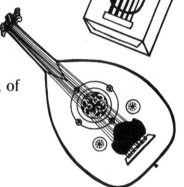

LUTES

Materials (for each student)

empty rectangular tissue box

5 rubber bands of different sizes and lengths

heavy wrapping paper, 14 by 16 inches (35.5 by 40.5 cm)

large wooden paint stirrer (available at paint stores)

tape

scissors

glue

1. Cover box with wrapping paper. Fasten with tape.

2. Perforate the wrapping paper covering the box hole. Fold paper inside hole and secure with tape.

3. Stretch rubber bands in size sequence over the hole.

4. Paint wooden stirrer. When dry, glue it to back of box as a handle.

DRUMS

Materials (for each student)

2-lb (908 g) coffee tin or oatmeal canister, end panels removed

chamois fabric, cut into two 14-in. (35.5-cm) circles

strong string

hammer and nail

wooden cutting board

construction paper or fabric, any color

glue

ice water

paper towels

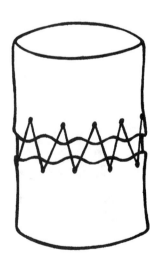

1. Measure circumference and height of coffee tin or canister. Cut out construction paper to fit around tin. Glue.

2. Lay one chamois circle on cutting board. Mark eight holes about 1 inch (2.5 cm) from edge of circle. Cut holes in material with a leather punch or hammer and nail.

3. Lay punched circle over the other chamois circle. Mark identical holes and punch or cut them out.

4. Soak circles in ice water for about 20 minutes, or until chamois feels rubbery.

5. Remove chamois from water. Lay circles between paper towels to absorb excess water.

DRUMS

Continued

6. While chamois is still damp, place one circle over each end of tin. Tie string to a hole in one piece of cloth, then lace through corresponding hole in the other piece, and so on, until all holes are laced. Pull string as taut as possible.

7. Tie a square knot to make sure the string won't slip.

8. Let drum covers dry for 24 hours before banging!

DANCING BELLS

Materials

(for one set of dancing bells)

2 strips of heavy fabric, 6 in. (15 cm) each

pinking shears

thread

8 large jingle bells (available in craft stores)

2 pieces of ribbon, 7 in. (17.5 cm) each

1. Sew four bells onto one side of each fabric strip, about half an inch (1.3 cm) apart.

2. Make a hole about 1 inch from each end of each strip.

3. Lace a piece of ribbon through the holes in each strip.

4. Tie a knot in each end, leaving 1 1/2 inches (4 cm) of ribbon on each side.

5. Tie dancing bells around wrists or ankles.

Robin Hood

FOR HUNDREDS OF YEARS, PEOPLE HAVE READ OR LISTENED TO THE STORY OF ROBIN HOOD, THE MEDIEVAL OUTLAW WHO STOLE FROM THE RICH TO GIVE TO THE POOR.

Robin Hood in History

The legend of Robin Hood became popular during the reign of cruel King John. This king owned many lands, while peasants and serfs owned almost nothing. While the king dined on wild boar and pheasant, his subjects died of starvation. To make matters worse, King John severely punished people who poached, or hunted illegally, in his forests—no matter how hungry they were. And King John still insisted on collecting taxes from his poorest subjects.

The English people disliked King John so much that a group of nobles wrote and forced him to sign the Magna Carta, a list of rules that helped protect people from many injustices. Some of the rights, or ideas about fairness, in the Magna Carta were used hundreds of years later in the United States Constitution.

The legend of Robin Hood may have been based on a real person who was sentenced to death for killing the "king's deer." This man supposedly escaped into the forest, where he gathered a band of followers. Robin's Merry Men may have been other outlaws hiding from King John's harsh laws. The character of Robin Hood came to stand for the plight, or difficulties, of the common man in England during this time.

The Trials of Robin Hood

According to the story, when Robin was still an earl, he went on a crusade with King Richard the Lion-Hearted. After returning from the Holy Land, Robin and other nobles were shocked to discover that King John had sacked, or taken over, their lands and homes. King Richard had died, so Robin decided to appeal his case to King John in person.

As he traveled through Sherwood Forest on his way to court, Robin was accosted and nearly beaten up by a band of outlaws.

Their leader, John Little, told Robin that King John had taken everything from nearby villages for taxes. Now that they had nothing left to lose, the peasants were going to take their tax money back by stealing from rich nobles. When Robin heard this, instead of being angry at the peasants, he became even more furious at King John. He decided to help the band of outlaws in their mission.

Robin taught his new friends to make and shoot bows and arrows. He taught them to set traps for animals—and rich nobles. The outlaws took the money from these nobles but never injured women or children.

Robin's childhood friend, Marian, warned the Merry Men about the Sheriff's plans to capture them. Because of this, Robin and his Merry Men were always one step ahead of the Sheriff. Eventually, Maid Marian and Robin Hood were married in a forest ceremony by Friar Tuck.

ROBIN HOOD

WAS HE REAL?

No one knows for sure whether Robin Hood was a real person. But at a church in Yorkshire, England, there is a gravestone that reads

Here underneath this little stone

Lies Robert, Earl of Huntingdon.

Ne'er archer was as he so good

And people called him Robin Hood.

Such outlaws as he and his men

Will England never see again.

The year of his death is given as 1247.

King John, by the way, died many years before Robin. The cause of his death? Eating too many peaches and drinking too much beer!

Name _____

If You Were Robin Hood

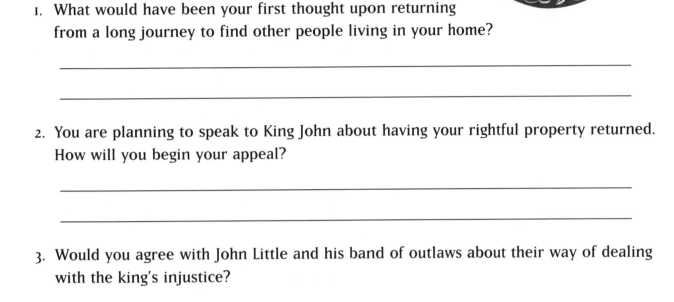

Use some of the vocabulary words at the bottom of this page to answer these questions.

1. What would have been your first thought upon returning from a long journey to find other people living in your home?

    _____

    _____

2. You are planning to speak to King John about having your rightful property returned. How will you begin your appeal?

    _____

    _____

3. Would you agree with John Little and his band of outlaws about their way of dealing with the king's injustice?

    _____

    _____

4. What would be three important skills to know in order to live in any forest wilderness?

    _____

5. If you had been caught, how might you explain your actions in Sherwood Forest to a jury?

    _____

    _____

Vocabulary

plight	majesty	band	poach	banish
legendary	manor	appeal	charter	peers
sacked	accost	illegal	grant	rights

CRIME AND PUNISHMENT

Robin Hood and his band of Merry Men were outlaws. Most of them had committed crimes against the King. Outlaws could not communicate with their families or friends. They no longer had rights to their property. Outlaws often did live in forests because they had nowhere else to go—and because they were afraid of being caught.

LAWS IN THE MIDDLE AGES

It wasn't hard to be an outlaw during the Middle Ages. A very small part of the population—the barons and members of royal families—made all the laws. They designed these laws so that they could hold onto their wealth and special privileges. They also wanted to keep tight control over the peasants and commoners. Common people had few rights and, if they were accused of a crime, not many ways to prove their innocence.

The Catholic Church also made laws. It controlled all court cases related to Church officials and property. The Church also decided cases involving marriages and wills. Some of the punishments for breaking Church laws were harsh. People who practiced beliefs different from those of the Church could be excommunicated. That meant they were not allowed to talk to or do business with their families and communities. They were not allowed to get married, or even be buried in a cemetery. This was very serious during a time when people held deep religious beliefs.

But the Church also helped people in trouble with the law. If someone was being hunted by a sheriff or mob, he or she could take sanctuary, or find safety, in a local church. If the person confessed to the crime, the Church would guarantee his or her safety until punishment was decided or the person could make arrangements to leave the country.

NEIGHBORHOOD CRIME WATCH

During the Middle Ages there were no police officers to patrol village neighborhoods. Groups of families would form small neighborhood crime forces, then elect one or two persons living in their neighborhood to police the area. If a person committed a crime in the neighborhood, he or she would have to be accused by someone living there. Then the local "police" would apprehend, or catch, the accused.

One way to prove guilt or innocence was by combat. If you had seen someone committing a crime, and accused him in front of the community, that person could challenge you to a fight. If you won the combat, the accused was pronounced guilty. If you lost the combat, then you were believed to be a liar and the accused was declared innocent. Few people cared to take part in violent fights like this, so few witnesses stepped forward.

Before 1215, people accused of crimes might be "tried by God" with a series of tests called ordeals. One popular ordeal involved making the accused walk over red-hot coals. The burns would then be wrapped in cloth. Three days later, if the burns were still visible, then the accused was believed guilty. If the burns were gone, then the person was declared innocent.

During his reign, King Henry II of England made trial by ordeal against the law. Trials by jury then became more popular. A judge and a group of community members would hear the case and decide whether someone was guilty. They might also decide the punishment. Countries such as Italy and France used the Justinian Code of Law. Judges and lawyers were given special training and a long education. These judges were chosen among the brightest people in the wealthiest classes. The judges, not juries, made decisions of guilt or innocence. They also decided punishments.

DIFFERENT DEATH SENTENCES

Capital punishment, or the death penalty, was common in the Middle Ages. People could be killed for not being able to pay their taxes or for complaining about a ruler. Nobles were usually condemned to die by having their heads cut off. Peasants were usually hanged for their crimes. Death by hanging took longer and was usually more painful than death by the sword.

Magna Carta Matchup

The Magna Carta granted certain rights to England's common man. It meant little to women, though, who still had few rights under the law.

Directions

Match each part of the Magna Carta in Column I with its meaning in Column II.

Column I

A) No sheriff, or bailiff of ours, or anyone else shall take the horses or carts of any free man for transport work save with the agreement of him whose timber it is.

B) No bailiff shall in future put anyone to trial upon his own bare word, without reliable witnesses produced for this purpose.

C) To no one will we sell, to no one will we refuse or delay, right or justice.

D) Let there be one measure for wine throughout our kingdom, and one measure for ale, and one measure for corn. Let it be the same with weights as with measures.

E) If anyone has been kept out of his lands, castles, or his right by us without the legal judgment of his peers, we will immediately restore them to him.

Column II

1) An accused person's property cannot be taken away without a proper trial.

2) Everyone will use the same system of weights and measurements.

3) Everyone has certain rights that can't be taken away or sold.

4) Before using someone else's property, you must ask the owner's permission.

5) No one will be asked to testify against himself, or given a trial without witnesses.

6) Everyone has the right to vote.

Name _____

You Be the Judge

During the Middle Ages, community members often decided how to deal with certain problems before the matters went to court.

Directions

Read each case below, then answer the questions. Compare your answers to those of your classmates and decide on the best judgments.

i. Jacob and Aradella

Two pig farmers, Jacob and Aradella, are engaged to be married. They live next door to one another.

One day, Aradella's prize sow broke down the wall of her pen, destroying Jacob's fences and garden. Jacob asked Aradella to pay for the damage caused by her pig. Aradella refused. After all, this is the man she is going to marry. They are going to share their property anyway when they get married. But Jason still insists she should pay.

The two farmers have now taken their case to the neighborhood council to solve the problem.

What are the main facts of this case? _____

What would be a good way to solve this case so that everyone is satisfied?

_____

ii. Ring Around the Armor

Gwen is lady-in-waiting to Lady Anselma. Gwen's son, Alexander, is ready to become a knight. Alex's father died last winter before being able to make his son's armor. Without the armor, Alexander cannot begin his training.

One day, Lady Anselma noticed her diamond brooch was missing. After an unsuccessful search for the ring, the guards noticed that Alex wore new armor and was announcing his intention to become a knight. When she heard this, Lady Anselma accused Gwen of stealing her ring and had her arrested.

What are the main facts of this case? _____

How can this case be solved? _____

If Gwen is found guilty, what would be a fair and just punishment? _____

CRAFTSPEOPLE AND MERCHANTS

The story of Robin Hood focuses mostly on peasants and nobility. But there was another class of people in Europe, the merchants. In the later Middle Ages, merchants became almost as powerful as nobility.

TRADES AND CRAFTS

Most merchants rented two-story village houses from kings or lords. The living quarters for a merchant, his family, and his assistants were upstairs, while the merchant's shop was on the ground floor. Since very few people could read or write, each merchant hung out wooden signs or large cloth banners decorated with pictures of their wares.

Craftsmen were people who made and sold specific goods such as food, clothing, weapons, armor, and candles. Other merchants and craftsmen, town nobility, and well-to-do peasants bought these goods.

GUILDS ARE BORN

In the later Middle Ages, merchants and craftspeople created guilds to protect their wealth. Guilds were groups of individuals who practiced the same trade, such as shoemaking, dye making, or cloth selling. During the 1200s, some large cities had more than 100 different types of guilds.

Becoming a member of any guild was a long process. At about the age of seven, boys became apprentices, or assistants, to master journeymen who taught them a trade. In return for helping the master craftsman, an apprentice received food, clothes, and shelter, but no money. Besides practicing their skills, apprentices ran errands and cleaned their masters' shops.

Once they had learned basic skills, apprentices became journeymen. A journeyman was paid for his work. In order to earn the right to open his own shop and become a member of a guild, the journeyman had to create a "masterpiece" that showed off his skills. This masterpiece then had to be approved by the guild master. Since craftsmen sold their goods after they were made, they could also belong to a merchant's guild.

THE GOOD OF THE GUILD

Guilds helped people learn trades so that they could live comfortably. Guilds also helped members and their families during difficult times by giving them money from a special fund. Over time, guild masters became very important community members. They helped get mayors elected and pushed for certain town improvements.

Guild masters also fixed prices so that everyone made an equal amount of money. The problem with this system was that it prevented fair competition. A person who worked harder than anyone else could not earn extra money, no matter how excellent his skills. People started to resent this after a while.

Eventually, guild masters became corrupt. They cared only about making a profit and not about poorer members of the guild. Over time, guilds disappeared.

Name _____

AT THE SIGN OF THE SHOE

Guild members wore emblems, or symbols, on their clothing that showed what they made or sold.

DIRECTIONS

First decide which guild each emblem represents. Then write each guild's wares (things they sold) using the clues in the Box of Wares.

A)  Guild:

_____

Wares:

_____

E)  Guild:

_____

Wares:

_____

B)  Guild:

_____

Wares:

_____

Box of Wares

> barrels and tubs
>
> pasties and chewets
>
> pattens and costrels
>
> ropes and truckles
>
> helms and bucklers

C)  Guild:

_____

Wares:

_____

Guilds

> Rope Maker's Guild
>
> Baker's Guild
>
> Armorer's Guild
>
> Cooper's Guild
>
> Shoemaker's Guild

D)  Guild:

_____

Wares:

_____

Name _____

SETTING UP A STALL

On fair days, merchants and craftspeople set up stalls to display their wares.

DIRECTIONS

Choose one type of merchant or craftsperson from the list on the bottom of this page. Find out what wares (or services) the merchant sold. Decorate your stall, using the directions provided below.

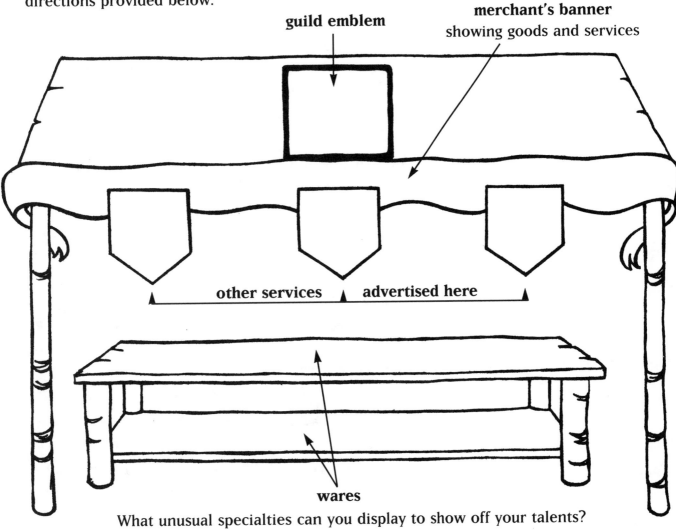

guild emblem

merchant's banner
showing goods and services

other services ▲ advertised here

wares

What unusual specialties can you display to show off your talents?

Merchants and Craftspeople

alchemist	candlemaker	fishmonger	shoemaker
armorer	carpenter	fruit/vegetable seller	tailor
baker	cartographer	glazier	tanner
barber	cooper	potter	weaver
butcher			

Medieval Money

The Barter System

Long ago, people used bartering to get what they needed. Bartering was a system of trading items of similar value. But there were problems with this system. For instance, people might not agree on what equaled a fair trade. Was one blanket worth a dozen eggs? Was a loaf of bread worth a pair of shoes? Sometimes a person had to trade two or three items to get one thing he or she needed.

Eventually the problems of bartering led to another system in which people used things like salt as money. In the days before refrigerators, everyone treasured salt because it helped preserve food. Salt was also hard to find, which made it even more valuable. Some communities used leaves, seashells, animal teeth, blankets, or feathers as money. The problem with this type of exchange system was that people often had a hard time agreeing on exactly how much money a certain item might be worth.

Coins and Paper

A group of Sumerian merchants came up with a better system. They needed something that would be accepted and valued in many different places, so they used silver. This metal was strong and long-lasting, so people used it to make many things. The Sumerians realized that they could melt down the silver into small bars. They decided how much each bar of equal weight would be worth. They stamped each bar with its exact weight.

This idea spread throughout Europe and Asia. Soon many people were using coins made from silver, gold, bronze, and copper. Each leader would have coins minted with his picture and other symbols that would tell people where the money came from.

The Chinese, who did not have a large supply of metals, used a system of paper money. This system was introduced to Italy by Marco Polo when he returned home from China, in 1295. At first, Europeans liked this. But problems arose because European countries were constantly at war with one another. This made it hard to keep track of who was ruling which parts of different kingdoms at different times. For this reason it was hard to figure out what value the paper had in different countries at different times.

CLUES TO HISTORY

Archeologists, or scientists who study items from the past, have found many coins from the Middle Ages in hordes of goods buried by people of long ago. These hordes were probably hidden before an enemy army invaded a home or town. Some hordes have included silver and gold coins as well as blocks of silver, jewels, and swords. Some hordes have included dies, the special stamps used to punch designs onto coins.

Archeologists and historians can tell a great deal from looking at coins. If they find many of the same type of coins, they know that people used one standard of money over a long period of time. That probably meant there were few wars and disasters during this time, or that a certain king and his family ruled for a while. They can tell if one country was more powerful than another by comparing coins from the two places. If a coin from France, for instance, used some of the same words and values as an English coin, England was probably the stronger country at that time. Fancier, thicker coins probably represent a more prosperous time in a country's history.

Coins found very far from where they were minted show that people were trading successfully with other countries.

Name _____

Minting a Coin

Most medieval coins were made of silver or copper. Commemorative coins were designed to celebrate a special occasion or person. These were often made of gold.

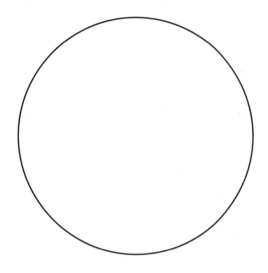 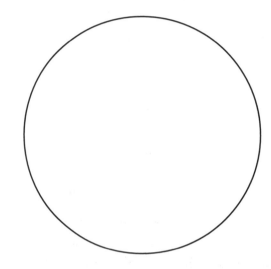

Directions

Look at the medieval coins on the previous pages. Use them as models to complete this activity.

To Design Your Coin

1. Think of a medieval person you find interesting. Write down some of the person's accomplishments or deeds.

2. Make another list that includes dates the person lived as well as events that happened during the person's lifetime.

3. Decide what symbols or pictures will go on the front of your coin: what the person might have looked like, the person's name, or a phrase that describes him or her. Make a sketch in the first circle, above.

4. Use ideas from your second list to draw the back of your coin. Decide in what year your coin will be minted. Sketch your ideas above.

To Make a Coin

1. Make a ball from self-hardening clay. Pound it out to make a flat circle.

2. Poke a hole through the top of your circle.

3. Use a straight pin to etch designs on both sides of the coin.

4. After clay has dried, paint with gold, copper, or silver paint.

5. Thread your coin with ribbon or string. Wear it as a medallion or hang it from a bulletin board with a report about the person on the coin.

Name _____

WHAT'S IT WORTH?

The main form of money in England in the 1300s and 1400s was the pound sterling (£) and the denari (d.). The pound is still used in England today.

DIRECTIONS

Use the chart below to figure out the answer to each question. Then use an almanac or ads in your local newspaper to answer the starred (*) questions.

A.D. 1200–1500	WHAT IT'S WORTH TODAY
One pound	$800 U.S.
One denari (d.)	$7 U.S.

A) In 1400 most people lived comfortably on about £ 7 a year.

In American money today, that equals about $_____.

* The average income of an American family today is about $ _____.

B) In 1320 most London houses sold for about 30 pounds.

In today's money, that equals about $_____.

* The average price of a home in America today is about $ _____.

C) The best carpenters in England in the 1200s might make 3d. a day.

In today's money, that equals about $_____.

* The daily pay of a skilled worker today is about $ _____.

D) In the 1200s a pound (lb) of soap cost 1d.

In today's money, that equals about $_____.

* The average cost of a pound of soap today is about $ _____.

E) In 1250 a pound of cloves (a spice) cost about 20 shillings, or a half pound.

In today's money, that equals about $_____.

* The cost of a pound of cloves today is about $ _____.

Special Project
Miniature Sherwood Forest

Use these ideas to create dioramas depicting scenes from the story of Robin Hood. Adapt these suggestions to create other scenes from medieval life.

The Forest

Materials

large piece of corrugated cardboard

twigs

pebbles

papier-mâché

newspaper strips

cellophane grass

brown and green tempera paint

1. Build up your forest floor by covering cardboard with newspaper strips dipped in papier-mâché.

2. Before papier-mâché is completely dry, sponge it with green and brown paint. Brush on some glue and sprinkle with cellophane grass and pebbles.

3. Use small amounts of glue to attach twig "trees" to base. Or build up thickness of twigs with papier-mâché; paint green and brown.

4. Use a small amount of clay to secure trees on base.

Robin Hood, Maid Marian, & Other Figures

Materials (for one figure)

oak tag

tape

pipe cleaners or drinking straws

scissors

modeling clay

colored felt or fabric, about 7 in. (18 cm) square for one dress or tunic: cord for tunic belt

beads, cloth scraps, cotton balls for decorating dress

felt and patterned cloth for hats; gauze for veils

To Make the Basic Figure

1. Use the size of your base to determine how big your figure will be.

2. Roll up strips of oak tag to desired body size. Secure with tape.

3. Use scissors to make armholes about the same height in both sides of the body tube.

4. Poke pipe cleaner or straw through armholes. Cut to desired length. (SEE FIGURE 1)

5. Roll up a ball of clay to fit snugly inside bottom of body tube. Insert wrapped pipe cleaners or painted straw legs into clay. Cut to desired length.

6. Make circles of clay for feet. Attach to ends of straws.

7. Use clay or small plastic foam balls to make head. If using foam, carve and color facial features. Use buttons and other materials to define features.

To Make Tunic or Dress

1. Fold cloth in half. Make a large slit in center of fold so it will fit over figure's head.

2. Fit fabric over figure; add a strip of fabric for a belt.

Fig. 1

Fig. 2

Fig. 3

3. Decorate dress with beads, cloth cutouts, and cotton "fur."

4. To make man's tunic, cut away bottom half of dress to form a pyramid shape. Cut fringes at the bottom edges of the tunic. Add a belt made from fabric strip or cord. (SEE FIGURE 2)

5. Use a small strip of paper to measure around the figure's head. Use this measurement to determine size of hats. Make a tall paper cone for a lady's henin. Add gauze or other sheer fabric as a veil. Or, use bright string or fabric to make a chaplet, or circlet, around the head. Before securing hat, you may want to add braided or loose yarn for hair. (SEE FIGURE 3)

To make Robin Hood's hats for figures, measure head as above. Cut triangle of felt to fit size of head. Glue two short sides together.

SHIELDS & SWORDS

Materials

oak tag

aluminum foil

construction paper, assorted colors

markers

To Make a Shield

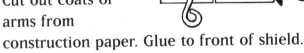

1. Cut shield shapes from cardboard. Cover with aluminum foil.

2. Cut out coats of arms from construction paper. Glue to front of shield.

3. Use ribbon for a shoulder strap. Tape strap ends to back of shield. Drape handle around shoulders of the figure.

To Make a Sword

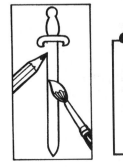

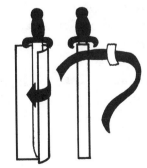

1. Trace a sword shape onto oak tag. Use pictures of medieval swords to determine the shape of the hilt, or handle.

2. Cut out sword. Paint. To make a scabbard, fit a small piece of oak tag around sword. Use a long strip of fabric to secure scabbard around figure's waist.

Answer Key

Page 13

Who Gets What:
  Dividing a Fiefdom
  The Green Knight
  got the biggest fief.

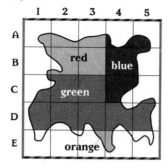

Page 20

Where in the Castle Are You?
  A) 3; chief porter B) 4; blacksmith C) 5; squire
  D) 2; soldier E) 1; queen

Page 37

Planning a Feast: Medieval Math
  1. 50 lbs
  2. 2 1/2 wheels
  3. 600 pickles per barrel
  4. 25 lbs of stew
  5. 20 lbs of turnips
  6. 100 cups
  7. 450 minutes, or about 7 1/2 hours

Page 46

The Herbal Healer
  1) Lavender and Rosemary 2) Sage and Chamomile
  3) Thyme 4) Marjoram and Borage 5) Lungwort

Page 47

Everyday Artifacts
  A) A flesh-hook was used to remove meat from
  boiling water.
  B) A costrel was used to carry ale or wine into
  the field.
  C) A pitchfork was used to lift hay onto carts.
  D) A spindle was used to spin wool into thread.
  E) A billhook was used to trim hedges.

Page 54

Stained-Glass Jigsaw
  When completed, this pane of stained glass
  shows three women gossiping, with devilish
  monsters looking over their shoulders. The
  lesson: No good can come from talking about
  others behind their backs.

Page 55

Treasures of the Muslim World
  A) 4 B) 6 C) 5 D) 1 E) 3 F) 2

Page 67

A Latin Lesson
  A) centum (100)
  B) audire (to hear)
  C) libri (books)
  D) vox (voice)
  E) adultus (adult)
  F) tempus (time)
  G) scribere (to write)
  H) curvus (a curve)

Page 68

Ye Olde English Poetry
  1) C   2) A   3) B

Page 80

Magna Carta Matchup
  A) 4   B) 5   C) 3   D) 2   E) 1

Page 84

At the Sign of the Shoe
  A) Baker's Guild: pasties and chewets (various
  meat pies)
  B) Shoemaker's Guild: pattens and costrels
  (Pattens were platform shoes strapped onto the
  foot; costrels were leather flasks.)
  C) Armorer's Guild: helms and bucklers (Helm was
  the word for helmet; bucklers were special arm
  gear worn by foot soldiers.)
  D) Rope Maker's Guild: ropes and truckles
  (Truckles were ropes used to hold mattresses.)
  E) Cooper's Guild: barrels and tubs

Page 89

What's It Worth?
  A) £ 7 x $800 = $5,600
  * The average salary of an American family today
  is about $32,000.
  B) £ 30 x $800 = $24,000
  * The median price of a home in America today is
  about $85,000.
  C) 3d. x $7 = $21 a day
  * The average hourly pay of a skilled worker
  today is about $11.40.
  D) 1 lb of soap = about $7
  * Today a pound of soap costs about $3.
  E) 1 lb of cloves = about $400
  * Today a pound of cloves costs about $48.

Resource List

William the Conqueror

(The Feudal System, To Be a Knight, The Castle of a King)

Children's Books

A Medieval Castle by Fiona Macdonald (Peter Bedrick Books, 1990)

The Medieval Knight by Martin Windrow (Franklin Watts, 1985)

The Usborne Time Traveler Book of Knights and Castles by Judy Hindley (Usborne, 1989)

Knights in Shining Armor by Gail Gibbons (Little, Brown, 1995)

Other Supplemental Materials *

Strategy Games Around the World (Edmark)
Software that demonstrates medieval games such as mancula, nine-man morris, and other strategy games. For grades 3–8

Knights and Kings (Entrex)
Software that poses strategic problem-solving situations. For grades 5–12

The Middle Ages (Queue)
Software that explains daily life, religion, agriculture, chivalry, the first three crusades, and feudalism in the Middle Ages. For grades 7–12

Destination: Castle (Imagination Express/Edmark)
Software that allows user to create electronic books dealing with life in the Middle Ages.

Castles: Seige and Conquest (MacPlay)
Software game with a medieval setting that involves building castles, fighting battles, keeping peace in the village, maintaining adequate food supplies, and paying off debts. For grades 3 and up.

Eleanor of Aquitaine

(Girls and Women in the Middle Ages, Noble Fashions, The Feast)

Children's Books

A Beginner's Book of Needlepoint and Embroidery by Xenia Parker Ley (Dodd, Mead, 1975)

Queen Eleanor, Independent Spirit of the Medieval World by Polly Schoyer Brooks (J.B. Lippincott, 1983)

The Medieval Cookbook by Maggie Black (Thames and Hudson, 1992)

A Proud Taste for Scarlet and Miniver by E. L. Konigsburg (Atheneum, 1973)

Other Supplemental Materials *

Annabel's Dream of Medieval England (Texas Caviar) Software that offers read-along story with electronic bookmark and comprehension game. For grades K and up

JOAN OF ARC

(Peasant Life, The Church, The Crusades)

Children's Books

Beyond the Myth: The Story of Joan of Arc by Polly Schoyer Brooks (Harper & Row, 1990)

Francis: The Poor Man of Assisi by Tomie DePaola (Holiday, 1982)

A Crusading Knight by Stewart Ross (Rourke Enterprises, 1987)

Other Supplemental Materials *

Rose Window Double-Sided Jigsaw (Past Times)
This 500-piece puzzle is based on the window from Chartres Cathedral.

Vespers From Notre Dame CD-ROM (Past Times)

GEOFFREY CHAUCER

(Ye Olde English Poetry; The Canterbury Tales; Games, Sports, and Other Fun)

Children's Books

The Canterbury Tales ed. by Geraldine McCaughrean (Rand McNally, 1985)

The Usborne Book of Juggling by Clive Gifford (Scholastic Inc., 1995)

I Want to Be a Juggler by Ivan Bulloch (Thomson Learning, 1995)

Juggling Is for Me by Nancy Marie Temple (Lerner, 1986)

How to Be a Juggler by Charles Robert Meyer (D. McKay, 1977)

Life in a Medieval Village by Frances and Joseph Gies (Harper, 1990)

Other Supplemental Materials *

Hazard: A Family Game of Skill and Fortune for 2–6 Players (Past Times)

Storybook Weaver (MECC)
Software that builds writing skills and provides medieval illustrations (among others) to include in stories. For grades K–4

King Arthur's Magic Castle (Orange Cherry/New Media Schoolhouse)
Software that offers a narrated castle tour, a jousting match, a maze, and a wizard's workshop. For grades K–5

ROBIN HOOD

Children's Books

The Forest Wife by Theresa Tomlinson (Orchard Books, 1995)

Robin's Country by Monica Furlong (Random House, 1993)

Lizzie Silver of Sherwood Forest by Marilyn Singer (Harper, 1986)

* All software for Macintosh, System 7 or later.